The Secret of Misthaven Light

KINDRED SPIRITS MYSTERIES

BETH CONNOR

WOLF GROVE MEDIA, LLC

Contents

CHAPTER ONE

In the Depths of Dreams

Ella Hayes found herself on the cusp of a world suspended between reality and fantasy. Before her, the beacon of a distant lighthouse cut through the night, a solitary pulse in the vast expanse of shadow and light. This rhythmic glow, like the heartbeat of the sea, seemed to whisper secrets carried on the wind meant only for her.

Moonlight wove through her chestnut hair, casting silver highlights that danced across her features. Her hazel eyes mirrored the wild spirit, reflecting its fierce beauty. She stood far from the familiar walls of her apartment and was drawn to the beacon's light. It flashed, and her heart kept time with its pulse.

The island itself emerged from the mist, a silhouette of rugged cliffs. It was an untamed land, with a solitary dwelling nearby the lighthouse. This was a place wrapped in the legends of those who had walked its shores before—echoes of laughter, whispers of sorrow, and love lost to time.

As she watched, a figure appeared from the shadows, a silent sentinel emerging from the night's embrace. His presence was a mystery, his features blurred, as if he were a spirit conjured from the island's soul. Ella felt a whirlwind of emotions stir. He was a whisper against the sea's roar, a curiosity that reached beyond the confines of her solitary life.

This was not the first time she had had this dream. Their fleeting encounters, veiled in twilight, wove a tapestry of intrigue and promises, pulling her heart toward a story waiting to be discovered and an island shrouded in secrets.

Dawn broke and Ella stirred from slumber, the remnants of her dream clinging like a second skin. It was in these dreams she wished to remain, for within their embrace, she felt a vibrancy, a life far removed from the waking world's dull hues. Here, in reality, a sense of isolation enveloped her, a stark emptiness that no sunlight could dispel. How she yearned to dwell where her dreams lent color to existence and she was never alone.

The days became a whirlwind of thoughts about the man and the mysterious lighthouse haunting her dreams. Life settled into a rhythm of eat, sleep, paint, repeat. Yet with each stroke of her brush, her obsession with the man and the unknown location grew, consuming her. Her apartment transformed into a chaotic collection of canvases and sketches, all depicting scenes from a place she'd never visited, and a man she'd never seen. She wondered if he was real, or just a figment of her overactive imagination? Each day, she delved deeper into this passion, her soul ablaze with the need to solve the mystery that intertwined her dreams and waking life.

One morning, as Ella was immersed in the swirls of paint on her canvas, a sudden knock at the door snapped her back to the present. A wave of annoyance swept over her. She treasured the quiet cocoon of her studio, her refuge from the outside world, and was annoyed at the interruption. Yet, as she made her way to the door, her heart ached with a twinge of loneliness, a reminder of her recent loss.

Her parents, who had not survived an awful car accident, had been the anchors in her otherwise solitary existence. They had always breezed through the walls she had built around herself, offering unconditional love and understanding. Her father's gentle humor and her mother's nurturing presence had been a balm to her introverted soul. Their sudden absence in her life left a void no amount of painting could fill.

As she reached the door, memories flooded her thoughts - the way they had always encouraged her art, their smiles as they admired each new piece, and the comfort of their quiet support. Their passing, though it had been a few months, still felt raw, the wound fresh as if it were just yesterday.

With a heavy heart, Ella opened the door, half-expecting to see their familiar, loving faces, only to be greeted by an outside world that seemed so distant now. She missed their gentle intrusion, the way they could turn her solitary space into a home filled with laughter and warmth.

Instead, she found Tanya. Ella always considered her neighbor Tanya more of an obligatory acquaintance than a friend. The older woman loved cats a little too much, and had a habit of imposing her presence on Ella. Still, Tanya's interruptions, though inconvenient, were never unpleasant.

"Hey, sweetie," Tanya greeted her with a sympathetic smile. "I haven't seen you a lot since, well... Just checking in."

Ella managed a faint response. "I'm fine. Just caught up in a new project."

Without waiting for an invitation, Tanya stepped in, her eyes drawn to the canvases. "Oh, honey, these are beautiful. What is this place?"

"Please don't... they're not ready yet." Ella moved to shield her work.

But Tanya, undaunted, continued to peruse the room. "You're looking thin, dear. I'll bring you some lunch later, okay?"

Ella nodded and acknowledged Tanya's impending return, her eyes following Tanya as the woman paused in front of the painting of her dream lighthouse.

"This scene, it has the feel of the East Coast, maybe Maine." Tanya mused, "Did you know many lighthouses there are rumored to be haunted?"

A spark of interest flickered in Ella. "Maine, you say?"

Tanya nodded, a small smile playing on her lips. "Yes, Maine. I've got a book about its lighthouses. I'll bring it along with your lunch."

Ella's response was measured, a careful balance to mask her growing excitement. "That would be nice." Her eyes betrayed a hint of the enthusiasm she was trying to contain. The notion that her recurring dream could be linked to an actual place sent a ripple of anticipation through her.

As Tanya disappeared to fetch the book and lunch, Ella's mind danced with images of rugged coasts and spectral lighthouses, wondering if the answers she sought lay within their storied walls.

Ella returned to her canvas. The brush danced across the surface with a life of its own. She was lost in the swirls of color that brought the scene to life, capturing the rugged beauty of a lighthouse perched on a cliff. It stood tall against the backdrop of a tumultuous sea, its beacon a solitary point of light in the encroaching twilight. Ella's strokes were deliberate, each one adding depth and emotion to the painting, the scene unfolding under her skilled hands as if by magic. Just then, the tranquility was shattered by the door swinging open.

"I'm back!" Tanya breezed in. Clutched in her hands were two mugs, the steam wafting from them carrying the rich scent of chowder. "Thought we'd stick with the lighthouse theme," she declared, a grin spreading across her face.

Ella's lips tightened. She hadn't expected sitting down with Tanya. Yet, the gesture softened her resolve. With a nod, she settled in at the table.

Tanya set the soup down before taking a seat. The book of lighthouses she placed on the table seemed to bridge the space between them.

Curiosity piqued, Ella reached for the book, her fingers tracing the title, "Shadows on the Shore: Unveiling Maine's Haunted Lighthouses and Their Forgotten Tales." As she flipped through the pages, a strange affinity for the tales and images of those remote sentinels washed over her. One story, in particular, captured her imagination—*the Curse of Misthaven Light.* The image if the lighthouse with the small dwelling next to it felt like a memory, as though she could wander its halls and climb its tower with her eyes closed.

This was it. The place in her dreams! She devoured the words, each syllable a morsel feeding her curiosity. The passage was brief, a mere whisper of lore about the Misthaven Light on a small island, nestled just off the shores of Bar Harbor, Maine. It teased at the notion of a curse, yet withheld the why.

Bar Harbor... With a sudden clarity, Ella realized her dream lighthouse was real! Her excitement was palpable, yet she held a part of it back, aware of Tanya's curiousity. "This lighthouse that looks like the one I painted, it's in Bar Harbor," she remarked, more to herself than to Tanya, her finger tracing the image of the lighthouse on the page.

"Oh?" Tanya picked up on Ella's interest, her tone casual. "Sounds intriguing. What's so special about this one?"

"It's… It's just different. There's a story here, something…unresolved."

"I love a good mystery, and you seem quite taken by it." Tanya smiled. "Keep the book. I have too much stuff."

"Thanks." Ella replied the gratitude clear in her face.

As Tanya's attention returned to her soup, Ella's thoughts were miles away, with Misthaven Light's steadfast beam and the mysterious man. They urged her to look beyond her life in Sacramento and to explore the connection tying them together.

Night after night, she was left with a maze of questions, but Ella sensed that understanding her link to the distant lighthouse and the figure was crucial to solving this mystery. In her dreams, the man was like a song on repeat, always there but forever blurred and elusive, shrouded in mist. His face was indistinct, but his lips moved as though he were trying to tell her something.

"Find me," he seemed to whisper.

One morning, Ella opened her laptop and searched for Bar Harbor, Maine, and Misthaven Island. A real estate listing caught her eye, sparking the beginnings of a daring plan. With her parents gone, she found herself untethered and questioning what held her in California.

This realization struck her with the force of a lightning bolt. The inheritance left by her parents was the key to a new chapter waiting to be written. With a clarity that surprised even herself, Ella chased her dreams to the rugged coast of Maine.

Maybe, just maybe, in the embrace of Misthaven Island's lighthouse, she would uncover the secrets that seemed to beckon her. This choice, fueled by curiosity, yearning, and perhaps a touch of fate, signaled the start of Ella's quest for self-discovery and the deep connection she felt with a place she had yet to see.

As soon as she embraced her decision, her life transformed with remarkable swiftness. She took a leap of faith, purchasing the cozy, furnished cottage in Bar Harbor without seeing it in person. The timing aligned with the end of her apartment lease, propelling her forward on her journey with a seamless transition.

In preparing for her move, Ella realized the simplicity of her needs. The essentials were her art supplies — the lifeblood of her creative spirit—and a modest selection of clothing for a few weeks. These were the tools and comforts that would accompany her into this new phase. Everything else she sold.

On the day of her move, she lingered for a moment in the doorway of her apartment, soaking in its familiar embrace for the last time. The cozy space was steeped in the sweet scent of dried lavender from the windowsill, intertwined with the comforting smell of oil paints and well-used canvas. Every corner, every shadow of the room, seemed to hold echoes of joy and sorrow from her past life.

Tanya spotted Ella surrounded by boxes. "So this is it?" Tanya asked.

"Yes, off to Bar Harbor, Maine," Ella responded.

"That's quite the journey. Ill miss you kiddo."

Ella's fingers played with the frayed edge of a cardboard box, her attention caught between the silent object and the unspoken words hanging in the air with Tanya. She chose silence, unsure of what to say next.

Tanya's eyes, much like those of her feline companions, reflected a deep understanding, an empathy that went beyond mere words. "Sometimes, our soul yearns for a new horizon, a change in scenery to stir our creativity," Tanya said. "Bar Harbor sounds like a place straight out of a dream. I hope you find what you're seeking."

In Tanya's words, Ella found a surprising comfort and an unexpected validation of her quest. As she turned to leave, she carried with her Tanya's understanding, a reminder that connections *could* be formed and cherished.

On her arrival in Bar Harbor, the sharp salty breeze and the distant crash of waves greeted Ella. The town unfolded before her like a scene from a storybook, with its cobblestone pathways, quaint cottages, and the endless dance of light upon the sea merging with the horizon.

Her new home was a portrait of New England's charm. Perched on a gentle hill, it boasted breathtaking views of the bay and the distant lighthouse. The cottage, with its weathered shingles, whispered tales of yesteryear. Roses and ivy graced its stone base, infusing vitality into its storied exterior.

Stepping inside, the cottage's warmth enveloped her—a living room, cozy and inviting, hosted a stone fireplace marked by the laughter of fires long past. Above, wooden beams cradled the ceiling, and the light danced on the polished hardwood floors.

To the left, was a kitchen painted in hues of the sea. The countertops were worn smooth by time and a porcelain sink overlooking a garden lush with wildflowers and herbs. A staircase led her to the bedroom that was furnished with a four-poster bed, cloaked in white muslin. It beckoned with the promise of rest, while a modest table stood ready for her sketches and blooms.

It was the three-season room, filled with natural light and offering an expansive view, that became her favored retreat—a perfect studio for her art. The wide windows not only provided a breathtaking panorama but also infused the space with energy. Here, Ella felt a deep connection to the surrounding landscape, which fueled her creativity and transformed the room into a sanctuary where her visions could take flight.

Living in the cottage was like becoming a strand in the fabric of a beloved tapestry. Every day brought new marvels, and the occasional nod from a neighbor while passing by hinted at the interconnectedness of this coastal community.

One bustling day at the local market, Ella found herself among a dance of sights and sounds. Fishermen announced their catch, bakers tempted with sweet pastries, and craftspeople displayed their labors of love. As she wandered the streets, a stall adorned with delicate seashell necklaces caught her eye.

Captivated by the craftsmanship, Ella complimented their beauty. The vendor, an older woman whose face was mapped with smile lines, responded. "They're pieces of Bar Harbor itself, dear. Each one holds a chapter of our seaside lore."

Ella was intrigued. She chose a necklace that seemed to whisper of the ocean's mysteries and asked, "Could you tell me the story behind this one?"

The woman began, "Ah, this one is a whispering shell. Legend has it that if two people each tell their deepest desires into it and then release it back to the sea together, the tides will carry their wishes to the heart of the ocean."

After hearing this, Ella felt a spark of wonder. That such a simple act could intertwine destinies intrigued her. While the tale seemed more like a charming fable than reality, it stirred within her a curious blend of hope and whimsy.

"I'll take it." Ella said.

As she reached for her wallet, a sudden jostle from a passerby sent a cascade of coins clattering to the ground. Flustered and a bit embarrassed, she knelt to gather them, her cheeks warming with a flush of awkwardness.

Just then, she was joined by a man who seemed to personify the essence Bar Harbor. His sandy hair shimmered with hints of gold in the morning light and his eyes were as deep and varied as the ocean.

"Let me help you with that," he offered, his voice a comforting melody of warmth and concern.

Their fingers brushed as he handed her the scattered coins, sending a surprising jolt of connection through Ella. It was as if a circuit had been completed, a current of unspoken understanding flowing between them.

"First time at the market?" he asked, a twinkle in his eyes.

Ella, still gathering her composure, managed a response. "Not my first market, just... not usually this clumsy." She could feel her face burning, hoping her embarrassment wasn't as obvious as it felt.

His smile was like a lighthouse beam cutting through a foggy harbor—bright, welcoming, and tinged with mischief. "It happens to the best of us. I'm Benjamin. Welcome to Bar Harbor," he introduced himself, offering a handshake.

"Ella," she managed, her voice barely above a whisper, betraying her nervousness.

Benjamin paused, as if expecting something more, but noticing her hesitation, he shifted to a softer tone. "If you're looking for tips about the area or just fancy a chat, I'm around."

After a moment that felt suspended in time, she found an opening to withdraw. "Thank you, Benjamin. I might take you up on that," she said, her voice steadier now, though her heart still skipped erratically.

With a small, understanding smile, Benjamin stepped aside, giving her the room she seemed to need. Ella turned towards the stall with a sense of relief and exchanged the money for the necklace. When she glanced back, hoping for a last nod or maybe to memorize his face for her sketches, Benjamin had vanished into the crowd. The space where he stood was now just an empty patch of cobblestone.

That evening, nestled in the snug embrace of an old armchair within her new cottage, Ella mulled over the day's encounters. The memory of meeting Benjamin brought a gentle warmth to her cheeks. His friendly chatter and observant eyes had offered a moment of comfort in the unknown landscape of Bar Harbor.

"Should I have asked for his number?" she mused to the room's stillness, her reflection in the window mirroring a shy smile. The idea of reaching out first was foreign to her, especially given the fleeting nature of their meeting.

As darkness enfolded the town, Ella's thoughts buzzed with a cocktail of emotions — excitement, hesitation, a budding sense of adventure, and regret for not doing more. She sighed, accepting her reluctance to act. Yet, the spark of curiosity about Benjamin and what he represented — a potential new bond — lingered.

She resigned herself to whatever might come, she trusted that if their paths were meant to cross again, they would. For now, she turned her focus to the adventures awaiting in her dreams.

CHAPTER TWO

A Fresh Start

In the quaint pulse of Bar Harbor, Ella discovered herself seamlessly woven into the fabric of its existence. The once alien landscapes now brimmed with inclusion and camaraderie. As she meandered through the cozy, narrow lanes, she felt a newfound happiness.

The inhabitants of this locale extended a welcome toward her that was devoid of any pretense. They embraced her as if she had always been a part of their close-knit community. It was in these simple, unassuming interactions—laughing together over steaming cups of coffee, exchanging knowing glances during the everyday hustle—that Ella discovered her niche.

In the crisp embrace of morning, bathed in the golden hues of the sun, Ella found herself drawn to the bustling activity at the dock. Here, in the salty air and the creaking of boats, seasoned fishermen prepared for their day. It was during one of these early walks that Ella, driven by a blend of curiosity and the thrill of adventure, broached the subject of a voyage to Misthaven Island. However, the captain, his gaze as weathered as the decks he trod upon, offered a gentle but firm refusal. "I'm afraid that's not possible, miss. The island's off-limits."

This refusal left Ella disappointed. The captain's words had a finality that discouraged further inquiry. Why was Misthaven Island enveloped in such secrecy? What mysteries did it hold that made it forbidden to outsiders? Despite the flurry of questions dancing through her mind, she felt unease—a hesitancy to probe deeper. She wasn't comfortable enough in these new surroundings to challenge the boundaries. This unspoken barrier cast a shadow of melancholy over her spirit, yet it also sowed the seeds of a deeper intrigue about the island and its untold stories.

Despite this setback, the village itself seemed to cradle her spirits in its embrace. A visit to the market saw Martha, the kind owner of a local bakery, with her hands cloaked in flour. Her eyes gleamed as she encouraged Ella to sample her homemade blueberry jam. This gesture showed the genuine web of relationships that Ella was forming within this community.

As Ella savored the delicious jam spread on a freshly baked biscuit, she found the courage to broach the topic of Misthaven Island, speaking through bites of her snack. Martha, with a twinkle of amusement in her eye, waited for Ella to finish her treat before responding. In a low, almost secretive tone, she said, "Oh, bad things always seem to happen there—too many people have been hurt, and it's fallen into disrepair. The authorities keep it off limits, but we all whisper that it's because of the curse."

"Cursed?" Ella echoed, her curiosity piqued even though she had come across this detail in her reading.

"Yes," Martha continued, leaning in closer. "Legend says that a long time ago, a sea captain's crew mutinied, leaving him stranded on the island before there was even a lighthouse. He perished from exposure, only miles from his own doorstep."

"Oh, wow," Ella responded, her interest deepening.

"But wait—it gets even more grim. The leader of the mutineers came back to Bar Harbor, and he claimed the captain's betrothed for himself. They were married soon after!"

Ella, intrigued and unsettled by the tales swirling around Misthaven Island, decided it was time to shift the conversation away from its eerie history. "I'll take a jar of this jam, and some bread, please," she said, eager to bring a piece of this warm community spirit back to her cottage. Martha, with a knowing smile, packaged up the jam and a loaf, her hands skilled and quick from years of practice.

As Ella handed over the payment, she felt a sense of connection to this little town. With her purchase in hand, she thanked Martha for both the food and the conversation.

As the day unfolded, Ella decided not to go home. Instead, she secured her recent purchases in her bag. The bread and jam, more than just food, now represented her connection to Bar Harbor's rich narrative, and its welcoming community. Despite the haunting stories that lingered like fog over Misthaven Island, Ella felt a reassuring sense of purpose and place here. Her steps meandered through the town's historic heart.

As she wandered, Bar Harbor unfurled itself like a well-loved book. Each street and building became a paragraph in its ongoing story. The cobblestones underfoot and the venerable facades around her whispered tales of days long past. This journey of discovery brought her to the doorstep of the town library. Ella found solace among stories and facts. The musty aroma of old books enveloped her in a comforting embrace. It was in this refuge, nestled among the chronicles of history, that Ella's solitude was shattered.

The unexpected sight of Benjamin, the man from the market, caused her heart to skip a beat. As he delved into the book with the focus of a detective on a case sent her heart into a frenzy, she couldn't help but state. Memories of their last encounter prompted an instant reaction. Ella, determined to avoid a repeat performance, morphed into an amateur spy attempting to navigate the maze of bookshelves with the grace of a gazelle. Unfortunately, her grace was more like that of a newborn deer on a slippery floor. This resulted in a less than graceful shuffle behind a stack of books as Benjamin looked up from his reading.

Her covert operation reached its peak when Benjamin, perhaps sensing a disturbance in the force or simply needing more books, stood up and stretched. Ella, in a moment of panic, executed a swift dive behind the nearest bookshelf, knocking a few books off in her haste, her heart racing like she'd just run a marathon.

The librarian, having witnessed the whole spectacle, approached. "Everything alright here?" she asked, her eyes twinkling as she glanced from the scattered books to Ella's mortified expression.

"Oh, yes, just, um, researching...gravity!" Ella blurted out. "And lighthouses," she added.

The librarian, struggling to maintain her professional demeanor, couldn't help but let out a gentle laugh. "Well, it seems you're quite the multi-tasker. Let me help you with these," she said, bending down to pick up the books. With a conspiratorial lean closer, she whispered, "You know, Benjamin is a great guy, and single. No need to hide from him. I would be happy to introduce you."

Ella, now a brilliant shade of red, could only shake her head, her voice having taken an impromptu vacation.

"You let me know if you change your mind." The librarian winked.

As Benjamin left the area, Ella dared to peek from her hiding spot.

When she was sure Benjamin was long gone, she stepped outside. The day's escapades replayed in her mind, painting a smile on her lips. Bar Harbor turned even the most mundane days into chapters of a personal novel. It had once again left her heart fluttering with anticipation for adventures—and perhaps more encounters with Benjamin (at a safe distance)—tomorrow might bring.

In the weeks to follow, Ella's seaside cottage became more than a home. It was a canvas for her story, each room echoing with the potential for new tales. The whispers of history and the call of the ocean through its windows set a rhythm to her life, inspiring her transformation. She carved out a nook with an ocean view, making it a haven for reading and reflection, adorned with a vintage armchair and books on local lore, in particular, lighthouses.

The process of turning the cottage into a place that reflected her soul was a journey of love, blending pictures and family treasures with quirky market finds. Sunlight and shadows played across rooms lined with handcrafted rugs and sheer curtains, crafting a serene setting.

Her studio, bathed in natural light and overlooking the sea, became the heart of her artistic exploration. Amidst paints, brushes, and turpentine, Ella found her voice. The sea and sky fueled her creativity, guiding her brushstrokes to capture the essence of Bar Harbor and Misthaven Island. Her lighthouse, once just a motif, became a symbol of her journey—both as an artist finding her path and as a soul connected to the coastal landscape that embraced her.

Ella's art led to a partnership with a local shop catering to tourists. They featured her lighthouse designs on postcards, blending Ella's vision with the community's charm. This collaboration extended her art beyond her studio, turning her creations into mementos that connected visitors with Maine landscapes. Through these postcards, her work wove itself into the fabric of the community, becoming a shared piece of the region's essence and heritage.

Amid Ella's creative renaissance, the mystery man continued to visit her dreams. He stirred a whirlwind of emotions she couldn't quite grasp. She resisted the urge to capture his image on canvas, instead pouring her feelings into her depictions of the lighthouse, making it a silent testament to the mysteries of her heart.

A revealing dream soon offered a clearer vision of this man. As the lines between her dreams and reality blurred more and more, Ella found herself in a dance of anticipation. Each night's sleep was a portal to further intimacy with this presence.

Compelled to unravel the mystery of this faceless man, Ella's days were consumed by her art, her talent blossoming. Yet, as dusk fell, she yearned for the dream world, for another encounter with the man who had become an indelible part of her soul.

Questions haunted Ella. Was she crafting a fantasy so vivid it overshadowed reality? Her quest for answers drove her deep into Bar Harbor's history, sifting through old books and faded photographs, desperate for a clue to the dream man's identity. Was it possible he was more than just a figment of her imagination? Did his story intertwine with the lore of the town itself?

Her art reflected this inner turmoil. Once tranquil, seascapes now churned with stormy emotions, her lighthouses standing as beacons of a desperate search, their light cutting through the dark mysteries of the sea. Ella stood at a crossroads, torn between the allure of her nighttime visitor and the grounding pull of the tangible world around her. As she navigated this twilight of doubt and discovery, the town of Bar Harbor became the backdrop for a journey.

Ella hadn't seen Benjamin again since the incident at the library incident. Maybe he is a tourist passing through? Yet, the librarian had vouched for his character, describing him as a "great guy." She wouldn't have spoken so confidently without knowing him. The discomfort from their last meeting lingered, a persistent fog of awkwardness that served as a barrier preventing her from searching for him. Ella couldn't help but mourn the loss of what might have been—a potential connection that was severed before it could flourish. Perhaps she had let a rare chance slip through her fingers. There had been something real between them, a spark of possibility that hadn't been given the chance to ignite.

The burden she carried wasn't solely because of unresolved feelings. Guilt gnawed at her for allowing the memory of a real man to fade, overshadowed by a figure from
her dreams. These fantasies infiltrated her waking hours,
casting a shadow that dwarfed the fleeting moments she
had shared with Benjamin.

The man from her dreams seemed to fill the spaces Benjamin left behind, offering an allure that was intoxicating.
This dream visitor, with no name and a face that eluded
clarity, became a fixture in her nights, stirring a longing
for something indefinable. His presence was a constant
reminder of the unknown, a challenge to the boundaries
of Ella's reality. As each night unfolded into day, the line
between the dream world and her waking life blurred,
leaving her to wonder if the emotions he evoked were as
real as they felt, or the echo of her own desires projected
onto the canvas of her dreams.

Caught in duality, Ella navigated her days with a sense
of disquiet. Her art became an outlet for the sea of emotions. This internal struggle, set against the backdrop of
Bar Harbor's beauty, painted a poignant picture of longing and introspection, a soul searching for answers in a
world where the line between reality and fantasy was ever
wavering.

Nights found Ella nestled in her reading nook, adrift in historical documents and town archives, searching for any clue that might anchor her dream visitor to Bar Harbor's past. Was he a sailor whose life was woven into the fabric of the town? An ancient keeper of the lighthouse? Or her own longing?

In her quieter moments, Ella wrestled with seeking therapy, questioning whether her mind had crafted an imaginary companion to occupy the silent, empty spaces that had grown in her life. The death of her parents had left her adrift, and the mysterious dream man had not appeared until after that devastating loss. Was this a sign of her psyche fracturing under grief? Could her decision to pack up and leave, chasing the phantom comforts of a dream, be evidence of her unraveling? She harbored regrets, wondering if her actions were a flight from reality rather than a step toward healing.

Yet, every time she considered distancing herself from these nighttime escapades, the undeniable pull of the dream man beckoned her back into his arms. His presence felt real. The thought of losing this connection terrified her more than the prospect of facing her mental state. It was a complex dance of desire and denial, where the fear of confronting her loss mingled with the fear of losing the one source of comfort she had come to rely on.

Ella's existence was a mosaic of dreams and waking moments. It was hard to distinguish between the two. Somewhere within this maze lay the truth she yearned to uncover.

The man's face became more distinct. His eyes held deep, untold stories, and his well-defined jawline added to his allure. He appeared to mouth words to her, but she couldn't make them out. She remembered the night when she first saw his features. This made her dreams feel almost touchable, as though she could feel his warmth and touch, as vivid as the sea breeze caressing her skin.

With each morning, the essence of those dreams lingered around Ella like a perfume pervading her waking hours. Her studio, quiet and observant, bore witness to the emotional whirlwind within her. Her canvases came alive with vibrant, passionate hues—fiery reds and deep blues painted with bold, enthusiastic strokes, each one more expressive than the last.

Caught in a wave of inspiration, Ella felt a resolve take hold. She faced the mysterious figure from her dreams through her art, her true domain. With charcoal in hand, she aimed to capture his image—the intense look in his eyes, the slight smirk on his lips, and the precise contours of his face. Through her artwork, she hoped to grasp his essence, to calm the storm he stirred within her, and to find the clarity she sought.

Positioned in front of her blank canvas, Ella aimed to immortalize the man who invaded her dreams and day-dreams. He had become a constant in the tumult of her emotions and stability in her inner turmoil.

The image expanded into an infinite landscape in her imagination.. She pictured the man, with the life and emotions etched in the shadows and light of his gray eyes—eyes that had beheld incredible sights and braved fierce challenges with resilience. His skin told stories of sunlit days and contrasted the darkness of his hair. A weathered tricorn hat sat atop his head, symbolizing the adventures and tales he carried with him.

With this vivid image in her mind, Ella's hand moved, guided by both certainty and skill. The charcoal became a tool of her intent, outlining the powerful jaw, the flow of his hair, and the unique traits that seemed to tell of ancient lore. Her lines awakened the depth in his gaze, so intense it felt as though he was there, looking back at her, their connection bridging worlds through the power of her artistry.

Chapter Three

The Historians Tale

Ella was on the edge of a defining moment, but sharing her research felt as intimate as divulging a secret crush. Despite the trepidation, she recognized the need for help, as her solo efforts to decode her perplexing dreams had reached an impasse. She caught her reflection in a puddle, wondering if her anxiety was as apparent as it felt. A quick adjustment of a stray lock of hair and a glance at her slightly flushed cheeks confirmed her suspicion that her usual calm demeanor was betrayed by a look of concern. "Come on, Ella, you've got this," she whispered to herself, trying to drum up some courage.

Upon entering the library, Ella was struck by a wave of self-consciousness. It felt as though the patrons had a supernatural ability to peer into her soul, witnessing her inner turmoil and the vivid dreams that haunted her nights. Her heart thumped so loudly she was convinced it could be heard across the room.

The librarian offered a small sense of familiarity in the sea of uncertainty. After remembering the librarian's previous acts of kindness, Ella approached the desk with a mixture of hope and nerves. "Excuse me," she began, her voice shaky, "I'm looking for information on the history of Misthaven Light. Could you help me?"

The librarian glanced up, her expression shifting to one of intrigue. "Today might just be your lucky day," she said with a secret smile. "Our very own expert on Misthaven Light is here in the library at this moment!"

Ella's stomach churned with dread at the thought of discussing her research so directly, and did not trust the woman's smile.

Leading the way, the librarian navigated through the library's maze of bookshelves, with Ella trailing behind, her mind buzzing with questions and concerns. How would this expert react to her questions?

They stopped in a secluded corner, and Ella's heart skipped a beat. In front of her, buried under a pile of books, was Benjamin. For a moment, Ella's mind raced with panic. It was one thing to face an expert, but confronting Benjamin, with all her unspoken feelings tangled up in the mix, felt like a twist of fate designed to test her resolve to its limits.

"Benjamin," the librarian called out, "this young lady has questions about the lighthouse."

He looked up, his deep blue eyes locking onto Ella's. To her surprise, there wasn't a trace of judgment in his gaze, only curiosity. She forced herself to regain composure and take a deep breath. The past was behind them.

As Ella blurted out a quick "Hello." Benjamin's fingers fidgeted with the edge of the book in front of him, betraying a nervous energy she hadn't noticed before.

"Well," he began, clearing his throat more times than was necessary, "I, uh, must say that our previous encounter was...interesting, right?" He chuckled, a little too loud, a blush creeping up his neck. "And, um, I totally forgot to ask for your number. It's not a usual oversight for someone who's supposed to pay attention to details."

Ella smiled, her own cheeks warming. "It's okay. I did not plan to bump into... well, anyone that day."

His fingers halted their dance with the book's edge. "And yet, here we are. What drew you to the lighthouse's story?"

She hesitated, picking at the corner of the book she held, searching for words that wouldn't sound too foolish. "I've been seeing... patterns in old paintings I've come across. The lighthouse keeps appearing, and I wanted to learn more. To see if there's a connection."

He regarded her with thoughtful eyes, a slow smile forming. "Misthaven Light has so many tales attached to it. I've always found it fascinating."

There was a silence, filled with the rustling of pages and distant murmurs of other library-goers. Both seemed unsure of how to bridge the gap that their shared awkwardness had created.

Finally, Benjamin ventured, "You know, discussing history in hushed library tones isn't ideal. Would you consider a coffee? Somewhere we can...talk?" He grimaced, his face turning red.

Ella grinned, finding his discomfort a relief. At least she wasn't the only one. "I think a coffee chat about lighthouses sounds just right."

Benjamin chuckled, his eyes lighting up. "Perfect. I'll pick up some books and papers from my place, and then let's meet at The Harbor Brew in about thirty minutes."

The Harbor Brew was a small cafe that served as both a coffee shop and a brewery. Ella was charmed by the clever wordplay in its name. While waiting for Benjamin, she browsed the posters on the community board. The place was alive with events, from art exhibitions to poetry readings and live music by local bands. She made a mental note to return one evening.

Within minutes, she noticed Benjamin tucked away in a corner, surrounded by a collection of papers and old books. He had been observing her as she explored, causing her cheeks to flush with a bright red as she caught his gaze. Ella approached him and was met with the sparkle of his blue eyes.

"Ready to dive deep into the history of Misthaven?" he asked.

Ella nodded, brushing a strand of her brown hair behind an ear. "I can't wait."

Benjamin adjusted his glasses. "Long before the lighthouse became the beacon of Misthaven Island, the area was infamous for its treacherous waters and cruel tales. One such tale is haunting."

Ella leaned in, her eyes wide with anticipation.

"There was a sailor, Captain Elias, known for his bravery and nobility. He was in love with a woman named Clara, a beauty who held the heart of many a man in Bar Harbor, but she only had eyes for Elias. That is until a treacherous first mate, Blackwood, took matters into his own hands."

Benjamin paused, letting his story sink in. "On a fateful night, Blackwood marooned Elias on the desolate Misthaven Island, leaving him at the mercy of the elements, with no hope of escape. With Elias out of the picture, Blackwood returned to Bar Harbor, weaving a tale of Elias's heroic death. Grief-stricken, Clara found solace in Blackwood's arms, unaware of his betrayal."

Ella's eyes welled up, the cruelty of the tale striking a chord within her. "That's devastating."

"It gets darker," Benjamin murmured. "Blackwood, realizing the strategic location of the island, spearheaded the construction of the lighthouse, becoming its very first keeper. He married Clara, and they lived on the island, forever shadowed by Elias's anguished spirit."

Ella shivered. "So, Captain Elias haunts Misthaven Island?"

Benjamin nodded. "Many claim to have heard his mournful cries on stormy nights, a chilling reminder of a love betrayed. The lighthouse stands, not just as a beacon for ships, but as a testament to love that was snatched away."

Benjamin looked pensive for a moment, swirling the coffee in his mug. The afternoon sunlight streamed through the coffee shop's windows, casting long shadows on the table, reflecting the somber mood.

"But the island's tragedies didn't end with Elias," he began with a solemn tone. "The curse of Misthaven Island, as some locals believe, continued with the next generation. Blackwood and Clara had a daughter, Isabella, as radiant as the dawn and kind-hearted. Many sought her hand, but it was Captain Nathaniel Hawthorne who won her heart."

Benjamin continued, "However, just when happiness might grace Misthaven Island once again, fate intervened. They found Isabella dead at the base of the cliffs surrounding the lighthouse. The whole town mourned the young beauty, and rumors spread like wildfire."

Ella's eyes shone with anticipation. "What rumors?" she whispered.

"There were whispers of a love triangle. While Isabella was set to marry Nathaniel, there was another who was infatuated with her, a man named Samuel. Some say..." Benjamin hesitated, weighing his words, "Samuel had feelings for Isabella that went unrequited."

Benjamin looked down, his fingers tracing the wood grain of the table. "Both Nathaniel and Samuel were accused of Isabella's murder at different points in time. The town was divided. Some believed that Nathaniel, out of jealousy, had killed Isabella, suspecting her of having feelings for Samuel. Others thought that Samuel, in a fit of rage and passion, might have committed the crime. But nothing concrete ever came to light. No evidence, no witnesses. Only an island haunted by the echoes of a love torn apart by fate."

Ella was lost in thought, digesting the heavy tale. The tragedies of Misthaven Island were more profound and tangled than she had ever imagined. "And what became of Nathaniel and Samuel after that?" She wondered out loud.

Benjamin sighed. "Nathaniel took over the lighthouse, a shadow of the man he once was. Some say he would stand on the cliff that Isabella fell from searching for her memory or spirit. As for Samuel, he became a recluse, shutting himself away from the world, drowning in his sorrows in alcohol."

Ella felt a growing trepidation. She cast a hesitant glance at Benjamin. The stories intertwined with the puzzle of her dreams. After steadying herself, she asked, "Benjamin, do you have any pictures of these people? Elias, Blackwood, Nathaniel, Isabella, Samuel?"

Benjamin paused, deep in thought. After what felt like an eternity to Ella, he reached into his leather satchel and pulled out an old yellowed newspaper article that had been laminated to keep it from crumbling away. A grainy image of a handsome man with an intense gaze appeared. The headline read: "Mysterious Death associated with Captain Nathaniel Hawthorne."

Ella's heart skipped a beat as she took in the image. It was him. The man from her dreams. But how? Why? The fabric of her understanding seemed to come apart at the seams.

Besides the newspaper article, a corner of a drawing peeked out. Ella's eyes darted toward it. "What's that?" she asked, pointing to the hidden photograph.

Benjamin tucked the picture away, a shade of unease crossing his face. "Oh, it's nothing," he replied, a little too quickly.

Ella's instincts tingled with curiosity. The energy shifted, and she could tell he was holding back. She wanted to press further, but decided not to. Perhaps it was a part of the story Benjamin wasn't ready to share. Or perhaps it was something else.

Ella's gaze wandered to the window, where a distant view of the water hinted at the forbidden contours of Misthaven Island. "I wish I could visit Misthaven Island," she began, "to feel its stories beneath my feet. But, of course, it's closed to the public."

Benjamin adjusted his glasses, an unreadable look in his blue eyes. He hesitated, as if measuring his words. "You know, there might be a way."

She looked at him. "What do you mean?"

"Next month," Benjamin began, choosing each word with care, "A group has asked me to collaborate with a paranormal investigation for a television show. They want me to provide historical context and background, and they've secured special permission to be on the island."

Ella's heart raced at the possibilities, the chance to be where her dreams and the stories converged.

"And," he continued, looking into her eyes, "perhaps you could join me... as my assistant?"

For a moment, the offer hung in the air between them, charged with potential. Without a second thought, Ella responded, the excitement clear in her voice. "Yes! Absolutely, I'd love to!"

Benjamin smiled, relieved by her immediate acceptance. "I should warn you, the team is quite... eclectic. There are a couple of investigators with some intriguing gadgets and methods. But the most interesting among them is a woman who is a psychic medium. She has a gift for communicating with the other side."

Ella leaned in, her intrigue deepening. "This sounds more fascinating by the minute. And maybe we might uncover some truths behind the stories, legends."

Time had a funny way of slipping away when engrossed in tales and the company of a kindred spirit. As the ambiance of the coffee shop had become more intimate with the dimming light, the voice of the server interrupted their historical odyssey.

"Sorry to interrupt. We'll be closing up for the afternoon in about 15 minutes." The young woman said. "But, we open again at 5!"

Both Ella and Benjamin looked around, surprised at the near-empty shop. They hadn't even noticed the dwindling crowd.

"I can't believe how fast the time has flown," Ella said.

"Neither can I. It's not every day you get so lost in history that you forget the present." Benjamin replied. "Well, that not true… that happens daily for me."

As they began gathering their things, the connection between them remained, and their conversation shifted from the stories of the past to their plans for the future.

Benjamin cleared his throat, a touch of nervousness clear as he adjusted his glasses. "Ella," he began, the blush in his cheeks making his deep blue eyes appear even more vivid, "today has been… unexpected and delightful. I've cherished our conversation."

Ella's heart skipped a beat, the sincerity in his words warming her from the inside. "I felt the same, Benjamin. It's been a while since I've had such a great conversation."

There was a brief pause, a moment where possibilities hovered in the air between them. Finally, with a smile that hinted at both hope and hesitancy, Benjamin ventured, "Would you be interested in continuing our discussions over dinner sometime? Perhaps explore more tales, or just... get to know each other better?"

Surprised, Ella met his gaze, her eyes reflecting her genuine interest. "I would love that," she replied, the corners of her mouth tugging into a soft smile.

Benjamin's relief was clear as he produced a card from his pocket. "At least this time, I remembered to give you my number," he grinned.

Ella's fingers closed around the card, her gaze landing on the embossed lettering: **Benjamin Hartley, Historical Researcher & Archivist.**

She laughed. "I'm glad you did."

Their farewells were filled with promise as Ella stepped into the dusky evening, clutching the card close.

When she returned home, her mind was filled with the captivating stories shared by Benjamin. The cottage seemed to echo with the remnants of their conversation, the aroma of coffee still clinging to her clothes. She hung her jacket, the smile from their meeting still dancing on her lips.

Her gaze wandered over to the easel that held the charcoal image of the faceless man from her dreams. She approached the drawing, her fingers grazing the rough texture of the paper. With a faint sigh, she dared to do what she had been avoiding—she gave the faceless man a name.

"Nathaniel," she whispered, the name hanging in the air, somehow fitting with the image before her. She studied the figure, the rugged outline of his form familiar, yet alien, in the soft lamplight.

After shaking herself out of her reverie, Ella moved to her bedroom, readying herself for sleep. As she brushed her hair, her thoughts drifted back to Benjamin. His bright smile, animated expressions, and the warmth he exuded all painted a picture of a man she was drawn to. His words, laden with passion and genuine interest, still echoed in her ears, and the historian's tales still sparked her imagination.

The fluttering feeling in her stomach, whenever she thought of Benjamin, confused her. He differed from Nathaniel—less intense, less mysterious—yet she found his kind-hearted nature and enthusiastic spirit compelling. His presence offered a companionship she hadn't realized she'd been missing. It felt pleasant, comfortable—different from the strange allure of her dream companion.

Ella was torn between the two worlds. Benjamin, with his tangible presence and affable charm, made her laugh and feel at ease. Yet Nathaniel, a figure that lived in her dreams, stirred within her an insatiable curiosity and an inexplicable connection that left her yearning for more.

"Quite the predicament," she mused to herself, letting out a soft laugh. She took one last look at the charcoal sketch, her finger tracing the outline of Nathaniel's face before she turned off the lights. She nestled into the soft embrace of her bed, anticipating the next dream, and closed her eyes.

As she drifted off, her thoughts wavered between Benjamin and Nathaniel. She was unsure of what the morning would bring, but for now, she allowed herself to be swept away into the realm of sleep, where the lighthouse stood tall, and Nathaniel waited.

CHAPTER FOUR

Shadows of the Past

The night was cloaked in an eerie stillness, an expectant hush that echoed in the silence of Ella's seaside cottage. She lay in her bed, wrapped up in the cocoon of her blankets, thoughts swirling around in her head. The stories Benjamin had shared with her played on a loop in her mind. The tragedy, the romance, the betrayal—it all seemed so vivid, like a movie playing before her eyes.

She couldn't shake off how closely intertwined her dreams were with Benjamin's tales. The stories of Elias, Blackwood, Captain Nathaniel Hawthorne, and the ill-fated Isabella sounded familiar, as if they were fragments of memories long buried.

As she mulled over the story's details, Ella found her thoughts drifting to Benjamin himself. His infectious enthusiasm for history, the spark in his eyes when he spoke, and the gentle, tentative way he had reached out to her. There was a magnetic pull towards him she couldn't deny, even if she tried. The idea of exploring whatever connection they had further was exhilarating.

A sudden chill jolted her back to reality. The curtains fluttered despite the windows being shut. An uneasy feeling settled in the pit of her stomach, as though she wasn't alone.

She sat up, scanning her room. Everything appeared normal. The familiar furniture, the pictures on her walls. And yet, something felt amiss.

There it was again, that coldness. A soft whisper, almost imperceptible, it danced on the edges of her hearing. Ella held her breath, straining her ears. The whispering drew closer and yet remained out of reach.

She nudged the blanket aside, the cool air of the room enveloping her as she swung her legs out of bed. With a sense of purpose, she moved towards the wall, her steps silent against the floor. Her fingertips brushed against the switch. The click resonated, a sharp and clear interruption to the quiet of the room.

Light flooded the room, harsh and unforgiving, banishing shadows to the furthest reaches of her space. Ella squinted against the sudden brightness, her eyes taking a moment to adjust. She had hoped the light would be her ally and chase away the creeping dread that had settled in her bones. The whispering persisted, a sinister sound from nowhere and everywhere. A crescendo of murmurs seemed to press against her, demanding attention, before it retreated as abruptly as it had come.

The silence that followed was oppressive, a heavy cloak that threatened to smother her newfound courage. Ella stood in the aftermath, her breath quick in the bright room, the uneasiness lingering like an unpleasant aftertaste.

She tried to dismiss it as a product of her overactive imagination, fueled by the haunting tales and the mysteries of the past. Yet, she couldn't get rid of the feeling.

After turning off the light, Ella tiptoed back to her bed, the darkness enveloping the room once more, but feeling a tad less menacing than before. She slipped under the covers, pulling them up to her chin. She nestled into her pillow and closed her eyes, focusing on the rhythm of her breathing. Inhale. Exhale. Each breath was a deliberate step away from the edge of her earlier anxiety, guiding her towards a tranquil state of mind.

As her body relaxed, she felt herself drifting. The transition was gentle, a seamless slipping away from the tangible world into the realm of sleep. And there, in the embrace of slumber, her dreams awaited—different this time.

Gone was the usual fog that shrouded her dreams, replaced by a clarity that felt almost tangible. It was as if a veil had indeed been lifted, revealing a dreamscape rich with detail and depth. Colors were more vibrant, the sounds more distinct. This new world beckoned, promising discoveries and adventures that felt real, each moment unfolding with the potent magic of the unseen and the untold.

The familiar setting of the lighthouse emerged, but with a new intensity. Everything was so much more tangible. And then there was him - Nathaniel, his name rolling off her tongue like a well-kept secret, as if it breathed life into the shadowy figure.

He was no longer just a faceless entity. He had a name. His striking features were sharply defined, his deep-set eyes reflecting a whirlwind of emotions. There was a marked change in his demeanor. An intensity that was startling overshadowed his usual calm and intriguing nature.

Ella's breath quickened as the pull between her and Nathaniel grew stronger. The space around seemed to shrink. The warmth coming from Nathaniel felt so real, a heady blend of musk and the salty tang of the sea. As their bodies met, the thin fabric of their clothes barely served as a barrier, doing little to shield them from the current that zipped and buzzed at their touch. The sensation was intoxicating.

What frightened Ella the most was not the strength of her feelings, but the lack of control she felt over them. They surged forth like a tidal wave, washing over her, leaving her breathless and desperate for more. This Ella was unfamiliar - not the one who always had control. No, this was someone else, someone who yearned and ached in ways she never thought possible.

"Nathaniel..." Ella's voice shook, a delicate thread of sound in the storm. She sought clarity and understanding in this whirlwind of emotion. But the dream offered no answers. The mystery of Nathaniel deepened, his presence a tantalizing puzzle that left her yearning for more, even as she feared the intensity of her own desires.

The face of Nathaniel in her dreams began to shift and merge. His visage melded into the softer, kinder features of Benjamin. The reassuring warmth of his smile, the depth of his brown eyes that always seemed to hold a secret, and the gentle cadence of his voice that made her feel cherished all intertwined with her heightened emotions.

Torn between the world of dreams and reality, Ella grappled with the difference between the two men. Nathaniel, the embodiment of desires, felt as real as the sheets she lay upon. And then there was Benjamin, the thoughtful historian who had awakened something different within her — a budding affection, a comforting connection. The lines between the men blurred, leaving her in a sea of emotion, wondering where one feeling ended and the other began.

As the first rays of the morning sun peeked into her bedroom, Ella gathered herself. The remnants of her dream lingered at the edges of her consciousness. She pushed these sensations aside, focusing on the day ahead. It had been a roller coaster of a night, her emotions swinging from fear to fascination, leaving her feeling more exhausted than rested.

With a sigh, she rose from her bed. Her body moved on autopilot, carrying her to the kitchen, where she set about making herself a much-needed pot of coffee. The rich aroma of the brewing coffee filled the air, a comforting ritual that promised a semblance of normalcy.

As she waited for her coffee to finish, she made her way to the bathroom. The mirror revealed the toll the night had taken on her. Dark circles under her eyes stood out against her pale skin, highlighting her restless night. With a heavy sigh, she traced the shadows beneath her eyes with a fingertip, feeling the evidence of her exhaustion.

Despite the weariness that pulled at her, Ella knew the day wouldn't pause for her to catch up. She grabbed her toothbrush, applying a stripe of toothpaste with a practiced motion, and swiped the brush over her teeth. She felt a slight jolt of alertness, a minor victory against the fatigue that draped over her like a heavy cloak.

When she returned to the kitchen and poured the hot coffee into her mug, she took a moment to let the warmth from the cup seep into her hands. The exhaustion was not just a physical tiredness but a deep, mental fatigue from the emotional ups and downs of her journey. She wanted to go back to bed. However, duty called, and with her coffee in hand, she grabbed the stack of watercolors she had planned to bring to the gift shop.

Mr. Elsnore, the show owner, had not arrived yet, so she handed them to the young cashier. She and Mr. Elsnore had agreed that he would select a couple for the postcards to be printed, and then frame and sell the rest on consignment. This arrangement, she realized, marked a significant milestone for her in Bar Harbor. It went beyond a mere transaction. It felt like a sign of acceptance, a recognition of her talent and contribution to the local culture. Slowly but surely, she was feeling like she had a place in this town.

She wasn't quite ready to head home just yet, so she took a detour and stopped by the local grocery store. The familiar jingle of the door chime greeted her as she stepped inside, the cool air from the air conditioning a welcome relief against her skin. As she wandered through the aisles, she enjoyed the simple pleasure of browsing the shelves, admiring the array of fresh produce and local delicacies.

She found herself lost in a daydream as she stared at the aisle of fruits, her fingers tracing the texture of an apple.

"Rough night, dear?" Mrs. Potter, the elderly clerk, broke through Ella's reverie with a knowing smile. The small community of Bar Harbor was more like an extended family, their warmth and friendliness so different from the she had been used to in Sacramento.

Ella offered a sheepish smile. "You could say that, Mrs. Potter."

"Ah, well. We all have those, don't we?" The older woman's eyes held a soft gleam.

Ella spent the rest of the day running her errands, the mundane tasks providing a much-needed distraction. Yet, the undercurrent of her thoughts, of her perplexing emotions, was omnipresent. Benjamin's smile, Nathaniel's touch, the burgeoning friendships - all of it was reshaping her existence in ways she had never expected.

As evening fell, Ella was back in her studio. Brush in hand, she stared at the blank canvas, her mind teetering between the world of dreams and the world of reality. She was an artist, lost in her own creation, the colors of her life now reflecting the hues of the mystery man and the historian alike.

The sudden, sharp trill of her phone jolted Ella from her thoughts, piercing the quiet of the cottage. Benjamin's name flashed on the screen. With a quickening pulse, a blend of excitement and nervous anticipation surged through her as she hurried to answer the call.

"Hello?" she managed.

"Ella, it's Benjamin," his voice flowed through the line, warm and familiar.

"Hi, Benjamin," she responded, her grip tightening around the phone.

"I was wondering if you'd like to join me for dinner tomorrow. At Le Petit Bistro, perhaps?" Benjamin's invitation was formal, almost old-fashioned.

Her heart skipped a beat. Prior to this, she had never experienced a proper date. Her experience with relationships was a few casual boyfriends in high school.

"Yes, I'd like that," she said, her voice steady despite the pounding of her heart.

"Great, I'll pick you up around seven?" he suggested, his tone filled with anticipation.

"Sure, Benjamin. Seven sounds perfect," she agreed.

After ending the call, Ella stared at the phone in her hand, her mind cycling through every word of their conversation. Tomorrow, she would be on a date. With Benjamin. The thought alone was enough to paint a smile across her face, her cheeks warming at the mere idea.

Her heart danced with a mix of emotions, a nervous excitement that felt both foreign and thrilling. The reality of stepping into this new experience with Benjamin filled her with a sense of anticipation, each heartbeat echoing her nervousness.

She couldn't help but feel a flutter of anxiety at the prospect of tomorrow. What to wear, what to say, how to act—questions swirled in her head, each one feeding her apprehension. Yet, beneath the layers of nervousness, there was a current of joy. The opportunity to explore this budding connection with Benjamin.

A chill night breeze rustled through Ella's bedroom, pulling her into a slumber that turned into another dream. The familiar scenery of the lighthouse on Misthaven Island welcomed her, the towering structure casting an ominous shadow under the moonlit sky.

Although last night's dream was intense, Nathaniel had always been a source of solace for her. The lighthouse, a constant companion in her dreams, never evoked fear. Yet, tonight, as she moved through the familiar setting, she was struck by a realization: Nathaniel was gone.

His absence left a void that resonated with her deepest fears. Could her feelings for Benjamin have driven him away? She roamed the lighthouse, peering into every nook, her calls only answered by the chilling echo of her voice against the stark stone walls. Warmth was replaced by a cold draft of uncertainty, casting an ominous shadow over her heart.

The dream's nature shifted. The sea turned tumultuous, its angry waves clashing with the shore. A storm broke the night's calm, lightning slashing the dark sky, painting the lighthouse in a threatening light. The curiosity that usually filled her dreams was now overshadowed by fear.

Compelled by an unseen force, Ella found herself on the cliff's edge, overlooking the raging waters below. Despite her inner pleas to retreat, her legs carried her closer to the abyss, her sense of safety unraveling with each step. Panic surged as the cliff's edge loomed closer. Was she being drawn to her own end?

Then, an unexpected hand brushed against her back, like a whisper against her skin. Whirling around, her heart caught between hope and dread, she half-expected, half-wished for Nathaniel. Instead, a stranger stood before her, his gaze filled with an intense loathing. The malice in his eyes plunged her into a fear far deeper than the unsettling dream itself, turning the experience from disturbing to terrifying.

She was jolted awake and sat up in bed, her heart pounding in her chest. The horror of the dream causing a shiver to run down her spine. Her skin was slick with cold sweat, and her breaths came out in short, ragged gasps. It was just a dream; she reminded herself, but the lingering sense of dread felt all too real.

As she calmed her racing heart, a thought occurred to her. She *had* to see the lighthouse. The need was inexplicable, yet compelling. She wanted to stand on the actual grounds, touch the real bricks, and maybe, just maybe, it would bring some clarity to the chaotic storm her dreams had conjured. This ghost-hunting adventure couldn't come soon enough!

CHAPTER FIVE

The Date

As the day turned to dusk, Ella found solace in her art. Her brushstrokes whispered of inner turmoil, yet offered calm to her nerves. Tonight's date with Benjamin wasn't just any evening. It was a step into vulnerability, a dance with the possibility of something new.

Her studio was a sanctuary where her creations whispered the secrets of her soul. As she cleaned her brushes and capped her paint tubes, a wave of satisfaction washed over her. She was surrounded by the evidence of her day's passion, the visible rhythm of her heart's labor. It was here, among her artwork, that she felt most herself, unguarded and true.

Among her pieces, the charcoal sketch of Nathaniel held an allure. She had rendered him with such precision and depth that it felt as if she had breathed a part of herself into the drawing. His eyes, deep pools of mystery, held stories untold. For a moment, Ella was lost in the gaze of this figure from another era, wondering about the life he might have led.

The sudden realization of that time had flown by snapped her out of her daydream. A quick look at the clock sent a jolt of surprise. It was later than she thought. Benjamin would arrive and she was still in her art-stained clothes.

Nerves fluttered in her stomach. As Ella moved to her bedroom, self-doubt pressed on her shoulders. Could she embody the woman she aspired to be? She wanted to radiate confidence, exude kindness, showcase her intellect, and share her sense of humor.

She rummaged through her wardrobe, searching for an outfit that could speak of effortless grace yet comfort her simmering nerves. Her fingers brushed against the soft fabric of a sundress, and she paused. This dress complimented her body and promised a whisper of elegance. It was perfect.

Ella faced the mirror, seeking reassurance in her reflection. The dress hugged her curves, showing the artist consumed by her craft and the woman stepping into a life-changing evening. Beneath the surface, her doubts lingered—was she enough? Ella allowed herself a moment of admiration. The warmth in her eyes reflected depth, while her hair cascaded around her shoulders like a veil of strength.

Yet, as she readied herself, the memory of Nathaniel's touch in a dream lingered, a ghostly caress that sent a shiver through her. It was a reminder of the complexities of the heart, the way it could hold on to a dream with the same fervor as a living person.

The soft rap at her door announced Benjamin's arrival. Ella, in a flurry of motions, fastened her sandals and tucked a stray strand of hair behind her ear. With a deep, steadying breath that did little to calm her fluttering heart, she made her way to the door. A quick glance in the mirror revealed a woman tinged with hopeful anticipation.

Opening the door, Ella was greeted by Benjamin's smile and eyes of such a striking blue that they lit up her spirits. "You look beautiful," he said, his voice carrying a sincerity that seemed to reach straight into her heart.

"You too," she replied. Realizing her response might have sounded too reciprocal for a compliment about beauty, she added, "Well, handsome, I mean." Pausing and blushing as the words tumbled out, she added, "Although men can be beautiful too." Her attempt to correct herself only deepened the embarrassment.

He reached out to her, his gesture so chivalrous it seemed to echo from a bygone era of knights and fair maidens. With a small, appreciative smile, Ella placed her hand on his arm, finding an unexpected anchor in his steady presence. Together, they stepped into the cool evening air and the world around them faded into the backdrop.

As they approached his car, Benjamin continued his role as a gallant escort. With a playful and somewhat exaggerated flourish, he opened the passenger door for her. This grand gesture brought a light laugh from Ella.

She settled into the passenger seat, sneaking a glance at Benjamin's smile just as he secured the door with a soft click. This thoughtful gesture sparkled with an unexpected depth. In that moment, their connection deepened, hinting at a budding camaraderie and shared excitement for the evening.

Their destination 'Le Petit Bistro', was a charming little restaurant that carried the aroma of authentic French cuisine right out onto the sidewalk. The subtle smell of roasting garlic and fresh pastries wafted through the air, making Ella's stomach growl in anticipation. The ambiance and soft melodies playing in the background set the mood for a wonderful evening.

Once seated at a cozy corner table in the corner, Benjamin couldn't contain his enthusiasm. He extracted an old leather-bound folder from his bag. "I thought you might enjoy these," he said, his eyes alight with excitement as he presented Ella with historical documents about the lighthouse and its keepers.

Ella was surprised. This evening was supposed to be a date, yet here they were, about to dive into history again. But seeing the genuine eagerness in Benjamin's expression, it was impossible not to be drawn in. His passion for the past was infectious, and she found herself eager to explore the stories he was so keen to share. After all, this was the reason she moved to Bar Harbor. There was something charming about uncovering secrets of the past with the most handsome guide by her side.

As Ella leaned in over the documents, the server approached with a pitcher of water. In a moment of clumsy timing, the man stumbled, nearly dousing the precious papers. In a panic, both Ella and Benjamin lunged forward, their hands brushing and lingering for a moment longer than necessary. They shared a relieved laugh at the near-disaster averted.

Ella's fingers then resumed their exploration of the documents' brittle pages, now even more aware of Benjamin's close presence. The archaic script and the pages' time-worn paper seemed to whisper tales of perseverance, mystery, and the intimate lives of those who had kept the lighthouse beacon burning. As the server, now more cautious, quietly filled their glasses and left them to their exploration, the history of the lighthouse keepers unfolded before them, drawing them deeper into the intrigue of the past—and each other.

Then, a particular image caught her eye. The sepia tones of the photograph didn't do justice to the striking young woman it showcased—Isabella, one of the lighthouse keeper's daughter. Ella's heart stuttered, her fingers trembling as she took in the image. Every line, every curve of Isabella's face mirrored her own. From the tilt of her chin to the intensity of her gaze, the parallels were unsettling. It felt as if she was staring at her own reflection, albeit from a time long past. Could it be a mere coincidence, or was there a deeper connection binding her to this mysterious lighthouse family?

Her introspection was interrupted by Benjamin's voice. "Doesn't she look like you?" He leaned closer, his eyes darting between Ella and the photograph, a playful smile playing on his lips.

She hesitated, still reeling from the discovery. "It's...uncanny," she murmured, trying to steady her voice. "I can't explain it, but it feels like more than just a resemblance."

Benjamin studied her for a moment. "Perhaps there's a story there," he mused, "one that's waiting to be uncovered." And as he spoke, Ella couldn't help but wonder if the story would be more personal than she had ever imagined.

Just then, the server arrived, poised with pen and pad, eager to capture their dinner choices. "I'll have the Soupe à l'oignon" Ella declared in her best French accent. Benjamin, with a nod of approval, chose the Coq au Vin.

"I have more information on Isabella, but maybe we should wait until after we've eaten," Benjamin suggested, his eyes flicking to the clumsy server before he cracked a grin.

"That sounds intriguing," Ella replied. "After the food, it is!"

As they awaited their meal, Benjamin offered a slice of bread across the table. "Try this with the olive oil," he encouraged.

Ella smiled as she took the bread and dipped it into the olive oil. She savored the crisp exterior yielding to a soft, airy interior, each bite a perfect blend of rustic simplicity and comforting warmth. This simple exchange, over a piece of bread, felt like an intimate dance of flavors and laughter.

Their food arrived, steaming and fragrant, and as they ate, the conversation flowed as freely as the wine. Ella, stirring her soup, hesitated for a moment before sharing, "My parents...they passed away recently." Her voice was soft, tinged with the pain of their memory.

Benjamin paused, his fork mid-air. "I'm so sorry, Ella," he said, his tone sincere. "I can't imagine what that must have been like for you." His eyes held a depth of empathy that made Ella's heart swell.

The conversation shifted as Benjamin shared his own story. "Growing up here, my family's history was always a part of me. It's like the town and the lighthouse are part of our DNA." He chuckled, a sound full of warmth. "Sounds cheesy, I know."

Ella smiled, shaking her head. "No, it's wonderful to have roots like that. To know where you come from. I've always wondered about my background. I was adopted, so my genetic history is a mystery to me."

Their meal progressed, with laughter and shared stories filling the gaps between bites. As they discussed the lighthouse and its keepers, their interest in the past seemed to pull them even closer.

As the evening drew to a close, the remnants of their feast were whisked away and the last sips of wine were savored. They found themselves engrossed in the lighthouse's lore. The tales, rich with history and mystery, seemed to weave around them, pulling them closer in a shared bubble of curiosity and excitement.

"Thanks for sharing this with me," Ella said, her eyes meeting Benjamin's across the table. "I've never met anyone who brings history to life quite like you do."

Benjamin's response was a smile that seemed to glow in the dim light of the restaurant. "And I've never met anyone as willing to jump into these stories with both feet. It's been a fantastic evening."

Pausing, Benjamin seemed to consider something for a moment before adding, "You know, we never got to the documents about Isabella, and I'd love to show you. How about we plan another day to dive into it? Maybe somewhere we can spread out the documents without fear of water attacks," he joked, recalling their earlier mishap with the server.

Ella's face lit up at the suggestion, the prospect of continuing their adventure sparking visible excitement. "I'd like that," she agreed, enthusiasm coloring her voice. "It sounds like a perfect plan for our next date."

As the words left her mouth, Ella felt a sudden rush of embarrassment for being so forward. Her cheeks flushed a deeper shade, and she glanced down, fearing she might have overstepped. But when she looked up again, the warmth in Benjamin's expression melted away any doubt.

"I'm really glad you think so," Benjamin responded, his excitement matching hers. "There's something special about sharing these discoveries with someone who appreciates them as much as I do." His voice carried a note of genuine appreciation, clarifying that the prospect of a second date was as thrilling for him as it was for her.

Ella's initial embarrassment turned into a shared anticipation. "Then it's settled," she said, her smile returning as she felt a wave of relief and happiness. "I can't wait to dive deeper into the history of Isabella and see what other secrets we can uncover."

They gathered their belongings and stepped outside. The chill of the night air was a contrast to the warmth they'd left behind, making Ella wrapped her arms around herself, suppressing the shivers. Benjamin noticed and offered his arm, a gesture she accepted with a shy smile. The walk to his car was short but filled with a comfortable silence that spoke volumes of the ease developing between them.

Again, Benjamin held the passenger door open for Ella, and she settled into the seat. "Thank you, Benjamin. This evening has been...more than I expected."

"The pleasure was all mine," Benjamin replied as he started the car. The drive to her home was smooth, yet charged with an unspoken anticipation. Every stoplight seemed to prolong the inevitable end of their evening, and each glance they exchanged was tinged with a sweet awkwardness, neither quite ready to part ways.

As they arrived at her home, the car engine's soft purring ceased. Ella lingered for a moment, her hand resting on the door handle, hesitating.

"Would you... like to come in?" Ella blurted out, her heart racing. "I mean, we could take a first look at the documents tonight. No time like the present, right?" Her words stumbled into the silence, her tone lifting at the end of the sentence hanging a question in the air. She bit her lip.

Benjamin's eyebrows rose in surprise, but his response was eager. "I'd like that," he said. "Only if you're sure, though."

"I am," Ella affirmed, stepping out of the car and leading the way to her front door. Inside, she flicked on the lights, casting a warm glow over the living room. Her home added an extra layer to their dynamic, and she didn't quite know how to act. She had never taken anyone home before.

As Benjamin entered, he removed his shoes, showing a respect for her space that Ella appreciated. She led him to the dining table where they spread out the documents.

"This document," Benjamin began, "contains the personal musings and thoughts of Isabella."

Ella's gaze met his, a thousand questions dancing in her eyes. "What did she write?" she whispered, her fingers running over the elegant cursive.

Benjamin leaned closer, his voice taking on a hushed, storytelling quality. "Isabella often wrote about her life by the sea, the ever-changing moods of the ocean, and her deep love for the lighthouse, which she considered a constant companion. But most poignantly, she chronicled her whirlwind romance with Captain Nathaniel. It was, by her accounts, an all-consuming love, filled with stolen moments by the shoreline, secret rendezvous under the moonlight, and dreams of a future together."

Ella's heart raced as he recounted Isabella's tales. She could almost feel the salt-laden breeze on her face and hear the rhythmic lapping of the waves against the shore.

Reaching into his bag, Benjamin unveiled an old photograph. The sight stole Ella's breath. The image showcased a marriage announcement with Isabella and Captain Nathaniel poised by the lighthouse. Their expressions spoke of love deep and undeniable. Isabella's beauty was familiar, while Captain Nathaniel bore an uncanny resemblance to the man who had occupied Ella's dreams.

The surrounding atmosphere grew thick. Ella's fingers trembled as she traced the contours of the faces in the photograph. "It's as if…as if I'm looking at reflections from another time," she articulated. "Their love story…it feels personal."

Together, they leaned over the papers, their heads occasionally bumping as they pointed out details and shared theories. The initial awkwardness of inviting him into her home faded as they delved into their shared passion.

Benjamin's eyes bore into Ella's, a shadow of uncertainty passing over his features. "It's strange," he began, his voice a touch strained, "how the past can have such a grip on the present. One would think Captain Nathaniel's presence is so strong that it might overshadow those who are here, in the now." His eyes darted to the photograph and then back to her.

Ella caught the hint of jealousy in Benjamin's voice and found it strange. An uncomfortable knot tightened in her stomach. As her dreams with Nathaniel pressed on her mind, she made a silent resolution to keep those dreams to herself. Sharing them with Benjamin would only complicate things. She offered him a reassuring smile, trying to lighten the atmosphere. "The past is fascinating, but it's the present that matters," she said, hoping to steer the conversation to safer waters. "May I look at Isabella's diary?"

Surprised, Benjamin blinked a few times before responding with an enthusiastic, "Of course!" He handed her the aged journal, its pages yellowed with time, bearing the silent witness of a bygone era.

As Ella opened the diary, the first thing that struck her was Isabella's elegant handwriting, flowing across the pages like waves. It wasn't long before she stumbled upon entries detailing her friendship with Samuel, described as a steadfast companion and a bridge to the most pivotal encounter of her life—meeting Nathaniel. Isabella wrote of Samuel with affection and gratitude, crediting him for introducing her to a soul whose presence would redefine her existence.

The diary entries became poetic as Isabella chronicled her growing affection for Nathaniel. She detailed their shared moments, the conversations that seemed to stretch into infinity, and the comfort she found in his presence. It was clear through her words that what started as a friendship blossomed into love.

One entry, in particular, caught Ella's eye—a page adorned with a delicate sketch of Nathaniel. The lines were tender, yet captured an unmistakable likeness. His gaze seemed to leap off the page. It was clear Isabella not only possessed a keen eye for detail but also an artist's soul. "Oh, she was an artist, too. This gets stranger by the minute!" Ella exclaimed.

Ella turned the page to find more sketches—candid moments of Nathaniel and Samuel, the lighthouse in the distance, the wild sea—all brought to life by Isabella's skilled hand. Her words danced around her sketches, a visual diary that intertwined with her written thoughts, offering a window into her heart's deepest chambers.

Isabella's descriptions of Nathaniel were not just of his physical appearance, but of that made him who he was—the strength in his convictions, the warmth of his smile, and the depth of his understanding. It was as though, through her art and words, Isabella was trying to capture the very soul of the man she loved.

Amid the sketches and heartfelt entries, Ella found a note about Samuel's changing demeanor over time, a subtle shift that Isabella seemed to ponder with a mix of confusion and concern. Samuel's introduction of Nathaniel to Isabella, a gesture of friendship, had given rise to a complex web of emotions, leaving Isabella torn between her loyalty to Samuel and her love for Nathaniel.

Ella closed the diary, her mind racing with thoughts. The parallels between her own experiences and Isabella's story were uncanny. The night stretched on, the documents between them a bridge to understanding not only the history they were unraveling but also each other.

Benjamin's gaze turned somber, a fleeting shadow crossing his face as he handled the worn photo of Isabella and Captain Nathaniel. "Isabella's death is the aspect of history most avoid," he remarked.

A shiver trailed down Ella's spine. Intrigued, she leaned in closer. Benjamin's voice grew softer, and Ella, eager to hear more, squeezed his hand in encouragement.

"When she was found," he began, pausing for a breath, "her friend Samuel had been to visit her on the island that day. According to court documents, Samuel claimed he was there to inform her of Nathaniel's supposed demise at sea. Samuel believed she leaped to her death. Yet Nathaniel hadn't perished, and there was no evidence that anyone had relayed such news to Samuel. Still, he insisted someone had told him."

Ella's heart tightened, sensing the sorrow that would shadow the beautiful love story she had imagined. "You mentioned this briefly at the coffee shop... but how did they find her?"

Benjamin sighed, his eyes drifting to a distant point. "Legend has it, she was found at the cliff's base, near her lighthouse. Life ebbed away in a tide pool. That's when the rumors swirled, especially since Samuel's visit coincided with Nathaniel's unexpected early return home. Nathaniel had hoped to surprise her. He was there when they discovered her body."

As Benjamin hesitated, Ella probed, "What rumors?"

"People started accusing Captain Nathaniel of pushing her, and that he suspected her of infidelity with Samuel," he revealed.

"But he was innocent, right?" Ella felt a chill as she recalled the face from her dream.

Benjamin nodded. "Yes, he was cleared, but the damage to his reputation was beyond repair. The dual blow of losing Isabella and facing baseless accusations shattered him. He retreated to the life of solitude in the lighthouse, which had belonged to Isabella's family, vowing never to marry."

Ella paused, processing the story, her thoughts in turmoil. Benjamin's hand hovered over his briefcase, then withdrew. "The other man in this story—Samuel," he added, voice tinged with reluctance.

"Samuel," Ella repeated, prompting him to continue.

"He was Isabella's closest confidante and friend, son to a wealthy merchant. Their families had envisioned a union through their marriage. Yet, Isabella's heart was with Nathaniel, and Samuel..." Benjamin's voice faltered, a storm of unspoken words in his eyes. "Despite being portrayed as merely a friend in their letters, rumors abounded. Some suggested his unrequited love for Isabella led him to extreme actions, while others believed his jealousy was not for Isabella's affection, but stemmed from a rivalry with Nathaniel."

Ella's eyes widened, the implications dawning on her. "Oh no," she breathed out. "And we might never uncover what really happened."

A heavy silence enveloped them. Ella's mind raced, the parallels between her dreams and the recounted history unsettling her. Benjamin's look was distant, lost in thought, and sensing the mood, Ella sought to lighten the atmosphere. She cleared her throat, shifting the topic. "So, any childhood stories you've yet to share?" she ventured with a light chuckle, hoping to dispel the somber air.

Benjamin's smile returned, a spark of mischief in his eyes. "Well, there was the summer I attempted to build a treehouse with my cousins. Let's just say it didn't quite go as planned."

Their conversation veered into tales of youthful endeavors, laughter mingling with the nostalgia of past innocence and boldness. Their mutual love for history and the arts shone through in stories of school, college, and career paths. Ella found herself drawn to Benjamin's sincerity and warmth.

The night wore on, and Ella mused, "You know, I'm really excited to visit Misthaven Island."

Benjamin paused, collecting his thoughts. "Actually," he began, "I've been coordinating with a psychic named Ashlyn. She's helped with my research before. And is part of the team we will join,"

"I can give you her number," he offered, his phone already in hand. "She is great at pointing you in the right direction for research."

With a gentle tap on the screen button, he sent the psychic's contact to Ella. Their eyes locked, and in that moment, the space between them seemed to dissolve, drawn together by an unseen force. Benjamin closed the distance, their lips meeting in a soft kiss. This stirred something new in Ella, a longing connected to the mysteries they were diving into together. They hesitated to break apart, grinning, excited by their shared moment.

The spell was broken by an unexpected sound—a loud thump, like a door slammed by an unseen force, sending a ripple of tension through the room. Ella's pulse quickened. "Did you hear that?" she murmured.

Upon hearing the unexpected noise, Benjamin stepped back, prepared to confront whatever was behind it. Ella's mind raced with possibilities. Fear gripped her—could it be an intruder? Crime in Bar Harbor seemed to be non-existent.

Then, as she tried to rationalize, wondering if perhaps an animal had somehow found its way inside. But her thoughts spiraled, and she landed on a more supernatural explanation. Could the ghostly tales be real? Was it Nathaniel's spirit? And if so, was this a sign of his discontent, or even jealousy?

After Benjamin had reassured Ella that the disturbance was likely nothing more than the wind, a subtle change washed over the room. Despite the scare, practical concerns surfaced. "Ella... I should go," he admitted, the reality of tomorrow's obligations looming.

Ella, caught between the warmth of the moment and the impending return to normalcy, watched Benjamin gather his belongings. When he paused, the space between them charged with unspoken words, he leaned in, sealing their evening with another kiss—a soft, lingering connection that spoke of promises yet to be kept. "I'll fill you in on the lighthouse trip soon, okay?" he whispered.

In response, Ella's heart fluttered. "Thank you," she managed, her smile bittersweet.

As the door clicked shut behind him, Ella was adrift in the quiet house, echoes of their evening together lingering like a half-remembered melody. New possibilities with Benjamin danced through her mind, each thought a step into uncharted territory, thrilling and daunting in equal measure. Yet, in the wake of his departure, an unexpected void spread.

Retreating to her room, Ella felt a tangled web of dreams and reality. Nathaniel in her dreams, once a constant, now jostled for space with the very tangible memories of Benjamin. Their images combined and shifted in her mind's eye, the ghostly allure of Nathaniel intertwining with the warmth of Benjamin's smile.

Lying in the quiet of her room, Ella grappled with the duality of her feelings. The prospect of Nathaniel being more than a figment of her imagination loomed large, casting a shadow over her budding relationship with Benjamin. Could she navigate the waters of a new romance while in love with to a ghost?

As Ella surrendered to sleep, the beacon of the lighthouse guided her through the murky waters of her emotions. Tonight, the questions could wait as she found herself lost in the fog of dreams, where both Nathaniel and Benjamin awaited.

CHAPTER SIX

A Heart Unseen

Ella's bedroom was wrapped in quiet, pierced only by the distant, gentle lapping of waves. Morning light seeped through her curtains, casting playful shadows across her walls. As fragments of her dream lingered, a profound sadness washed over her.

Nathaniel, with his deep, yearning eyes, felt more tangible than ever. He reached out across time and space. His eyes, brimming with a timeless sorrow, drew her in, even if they were anchored in a far-off past.

Wrapped in her tangled sheets, Ella could still sense his stare. The emotions that surged within her felt overwhelmingly real. They threatened to overshadow the fledgling feelings she harbored for Benjamin.

The idea of therapy crossed her mind once more. It didn't seem like such a bad idea, especially with the unresolved grief from her parents' passing still hanging over her. But discussing her dream-induced infatuation? She wasn't ready for Nathaniel to fade into oblivion. He called to her in a way she couldn't ignore.

Then she remembered Benjamin's suggestion to consult Ashlyn Alden, a psychic. Her phone lay within easy reach on the bedside table. Benjamin had already spoken to Ashlyn about her situation. Torn, Ella pondered over her next move. She sought answers, yet how could she tell such intimate dreams to a stranger? Moreover, this stranger was Benjamin's friend.

She pictured herself on the phone, her voice breaking as she tried to articulate her dreams to Ashlyn. Heat crept into her cheeks at the thought. Would Ashlyn dismiss her as just another lovesick ghost hunter, reading too much into her nighttime fantasies? And if Ashlyn believed her, would she end up discussing it with Benjamin? This possibility made Ella even more hesitant.

She put the phone, deciding not to call—at least not yet. But as the morning glow intensified, filling her room with light and dispelling the shadows, Ella felt herself unraveling.

The weather over Bar Harbor had draped itself in a cloak of dreariness for days, the persistent drizzle and fog that seemed to seep into the bones and the hearts of its inhabitants. Within the cozy confines of Ella's living room, she and Benjamin found solace from the grey skies, surrounded by history.

Benjamin opened a folder he had prepared for the ghost hunting expedition, revealing the faded images of those whose stories were intertwined with the island's lore. "Let's start with Captain Elias Thornton," he began, pointing to an image of a man whose gaze was as deep as the ocean he had once mastered. "Thornton was born in 1823 and became a legend on the seas. However, his story took a tragic turn when he was lost in the very waters he loved. It's said his spirit still wanders the shores of Misthaven Island, perhaps unable to leave the love he left behind."

Ella, drawn into the tale, leaned in. "And that love would be Clara?" she ventured, her voice a soft echo in the room filled with the sound of rain against the windows.

"Yes, that's where the story becomes even more entangled," Benjamin replied, shifting to another photograph, and practicing for his camera time. "Thornton was betrothed to a woman named Clara, who had a remarkable spirit and beauty, but fate had other plans. All too soon after Thornton's death, she found solace and eventually love with Armand Blackwood."

"Blackwood?" Ella's brow furrowed. "Was the man that marooned Elias Thorton, right?"

"Exactly," Benjamin confirmed, revealing a portrait of Armand Blackwood, a man whose eyes carried deep secrets. "Armand and Clara married and had one daughter, Isabella. This island was their world, and the lighthouse was their beacon. But it was also the setting for a love story that would echo through the ages."

He then turned to a delicate, age-worn picture of Isabella Blackwood. It was still strange to Ella how much this woman resembled her. "Isabella grew up in the lighthouse's shadow, nurtured by the loving, vigilant care of her parents. Both her mother, Clara, and her father played pivotal roles in her upbringing, ensuring she was well-loved and protected. However, tragedy struck early when Clara passed away, leaving a young Isabella to navigate the world with only her father's guidance. Despite this loss, her spirit remained unbroken, and her life took a poignant turn when Nathaniel Hawthorne entered her life, capturing her heart with a story all their own."

Ella traced her finger over Isabella's image. "So, Hawthorne and Isabella were the true loves of this tale," she murmured, lost in thought.

"Yes, but as with all the great tales, tragedy was never far behind. Their union, destined for happiness, was cut short by circumstances beyond their control. Isabella's untimely death. Now, it's as if Misthaven itself holds their memories, whispering their names with every gust of wind and crash of wave against the shore."

"That sounded amazing. The camera is going to love you!" She paused. "do you know why we are reaching out to them?" Ella asked, her voice barely above the crackle of the fireplace.

Benjamin closed the folder, his eyes meeting Ella's. "Their stories are unresolved, their spirits restless. By connecting with them, we not only uncover the mysteries of the past, but perhaps bring peace to those who have been silent for too long."

As the rain intensified outside, blurring the world into a monochrome of grey, Ella felt the magnitude of their task deepen. Within the safety of her living room, she and Benjamin were not chasing shadows for a ghost hunter's project. They were threading through the fabric of history itself.

Ella pondered the intertwining tales of Nathaniel, Isabella, Elias, and the others whose spirits still whispered through the island. She realized this endeavor transcended the more than uncovering ghostly tales. It mirrored her own search for answers, a journey through her personal labyrinth of questions and curiosities about the past.

In pursuing understanding these long-gone lives, Ella realized she might also illuminate the darker corners of her own story. The project offered a unique lens through which to view her own mysteries. Perhaps this journey might hold keys to unlocking parts of her own history and identity.

Ella and Benjamin found themselves caught in a whirlwind of preparation, their days filled with a sense of anticipation for the investigation. Beneath the surface, the undercurrents of a budding romance wove through their interactions. Yet, as much as Benjamin inhabited her waking thoughts, Nathaniel still haunted Ella's dreams.

One evening, as they sat side by side on Ella's porch, watching the soft glow of twilight, Benjamin's hand found Ella's. The warmth of his touch spiraled up her arm. "You seem distant," he noted.

Ella hesitated, caught between the desire to share her dreams and the fear of what revealing them might entail.

She opted for half-truths. "Just lost in thought," she murmured, her gaze fixed on the fading light.

The moment of evasion cast a shadow over Benjamin's features. However, their conversation was halted by the ring of his phone. "It's Ashlyn. I need to take this," he excused himself, stepping away with a glance that left Ella feeling isolated.

From her vantage point, Ella watched him, noting the ease and animation that flowed into his conversation with Ashlyn. A pang of jealousy, sharp and unexpected, pierced through her, leaving her unsettled and questioning the intensity of her feelings. Why did this glimpse into Benjamin's world, shared with someone else, stir such a storm within her?

Ella turned her attention back to the horizon, seeking solace in the evening's beauty. She let the moment—a whisper of the sea, the chirping of the crickets, and the caress of the breeze—enfold her. If nothing else the it dispelled the unwelcome surge of jealousy.

When Benjamin ended the call and returned, the atmosphere between them felt changed. The earlier warmth seemed to have dulled, replaced by a quiet tension. Both seemed lost in their own worlds, the chasm of unspoken thoughts and feelings creating a distance that wasn't there before.

Benjamin cleared his throat, breaking the silence that had settled between them. "I should go," he said, avoiding direct eye contact.

Ella nodded, unspoken words between them pressing down on her chest. "Can I keep the files for tonight?" she asked, gesturing to the pile of documents they had been going through earlier. She hoped to lose herself in the work, to quiet the turmoil of her emotions.

Benjamin hesitated, his gaze flitting between the files and then back to Ella. "I... yes, of course," he replied, though reluctance tinged his voice. "Just take care of them, okay? They're quite valuable."

Ella offered a small smile. "I promise. I'll keep them safe."

They exchanged a few more words. A formal veneer of politeness amid the strange tension. As the door closed behind Benjamin, Ella was left with the files, and the haunting image of Nathaniel, whose presence in her dreams, added layers of complexity to her emotions.

Ella seized the moment to delve into a treasure she had been yearning to explore in private: Isabella's journal. The personal artifact, a window into the life of her counterpart from the 1800s, was nothing short of astonishing. The leather-bound journal, its pages yellowed with age, lay in her hands like a delicate piece of history, eager to unveil its secrets.

Ella's fingers traced the edges of the journal's pages, now more familiar to her touch, as she settled into the armchair. This time, however, she bypassed the early entries she had already poured over. Instead, she went to a series of delicate sketches nestled between the written accounts—a gallery of Nathaniel's visage captured in Isabella's hand. These drawings were intimate and revealing, each stroke of the pencil whispering secrets of love.

As she delved deeper, the journal told of Isabella's life in a way that was less about the words on the page and more about the emotions. Isabella's unease and the sense of being watched by something unseen were now familiar tales to Ella. Yet, setting, with the soft hum of the sea beyond, she found herself enveloped in the warmth of Isabella's more personal revelations (and encounters) Nathaniel.

Ella blushed as she pored over entries nestled between sketches of Nathaniel in Isabella's journal. These sections were full of Isabella's feelings, portraying a side of the past Ella had never imagined. She had always pictured women of that era as reserved and devout, their lives laced within the confines of propriety. Yet here was Isabella, expressing a passion and depth of feeling that was surprising.

More intriguing were the hints of their closeness, the intimacies shared in the quiet moments away from prying eyes. These were not the escapades of romance novels, but hinted at a depth of relationship Ella hadn't expected.

Isabella's yearning during Nathaniel's absences was obvious. Yet, even in these moments of vulnerability, there was a strength in her longing, a candid acknowledgment of desire and affection that made Ella's cheeks warm with a mix of embarrassment.

Through these revelations, Ella discovered a connection to Isabella. She realized the past was not a world of restraint and repression, but was as vivid and full of emotion as her own. Isabella's expressions of love painted a portrait of a woman bold in her emotional honesty, challenging Ella's preconceptions and inviting her to view the past through a new lens.

That night, Ella's bed felt vast and empty. As she closed her eyes, Nathaniel's image greeted her, his gaze fervent yet veiled with a melancholy she couldn't decipher. There seemed to be an air of distance, a chasm growing between them.

This growing rift in her dreams mirrored the distance that had crept into her waking world with Benjamin. Just as Nathaniel's image receded into subconscious, the warmth and immediacy of her connection with Benjamin seemed to ebb away, leaving her adrift in both worlds—each filled with its own brand of silence and yearning.

Within the dream, Nathaniel cradled her cheek, his touch both a sanctuary and a promise. The fervor in these moments eclipsed any physical connection she'd felt with Benjamin. It felt like Nathaniel entrusted her with his being.

But with every tender touch, Ella sensed Nathaniel's presence diminishing. Where he once stood commanding, he was fading into the background. His figure dimming, like an old photograph losing its contrast. It was as if he was receding into the foggy recesses of her mind, retreating to that shadowy corner where he first materialized.

The next morning, Ella rose with the first light, her dreams still clinging to her. She had slipped out of bed, opting for a quick change into a pair of underwear and throwing on an oversized t-shirt rather than a full outfit. Her studio always called to her, especially when emotions ran high. It was her sanctuary. Here, surrounded by the hush of morning and the familiar scent of paint and charcoal, her thoughts flowed onto the canvas. The portrait she now drew with such fervor was that of Nathaniel.

Engrossed in her art, the sudden creak of the studio door jolted Ella from her introspection. The sight of Benjamin caught her off guard, especially given her scant attire. Benjamin's eyes, however, held no judgment but an unspoken apology. In his hand, a bouquet seemed like a peace offering, a gesture to mend the rift that had grown between them.

"You scared me," she whispered, her previous discomfort forgotten. "I wasn't expecting you."

He grinned, yet as his gaze fell upon the portrait, there was a flash of intensity. "The captain from the lighthouse photographs?" he inquired, voice strained.

Ella felt a mix of pride and unease. "I felt inspired," she said, trying to deflect from the tension that filled the space between them. His eyes darkened, and a silence settled. Hoping to dissipate the heaviness, she suggested, "Let's go to the living room?"

As they moved, Ella sensed a shift in Benjamin. His arm wrapped around her, pulling her close. His touch, usually comforting, felt possessive now.

Benjamin's grip tightened on Ella as he spun her around and pushed her forward.

"Benjamin..." she began

"You're mine," he rasped into her ear, his voice dark and edged with dominance. "Only mine."

Ella's heart raced as the words filled her head and the hairs on the back of her neck stood on end. *Does he somehow know about Nathaniel?* It felt impossible, but the grip of his hands told another story. The need to confront this unexpected side of Benjamin became overwhelming.

She twisted and found herself face-to-face with him. His eyes were tempestuous and black with intensity. Their depth held a swirling mix of emotions she couldn't decode, but what was unmistakable was the raw desire and urgency. The intensity felt misplaced, too abrupt. This wasn't the Benjamin she knew.

He twitched, as though snapping back to the man she knew. Benjamin's confusion was apparent in his clear blue eyes. Ella tugged at the hem of her t-shirt, trying to cover herself.

"Yes, Benjamin, you're the only one. But..." Ella's voice wavered.

The moment bore down on him. "Ella, I... I can't recall... I'm so sorry." He paused, regret in his gaze. "I don't understand what just took over."

The distance between them grew as he shuffled, awkward and disheveled, towards the door. "Maybe I should go," he whispered, his voice thick with mixed emotions.

"No, Benjamin, wait," she called out with a half-hearted attempt to keep him from leaving, but he was already through the door.

From her vantage point, she watched him take out his phone and start dialing. Could he be calling Ashlyn? The mere thought added a sting to the tumult of emotions swirling within her. Was she the one he'd sought now? The idea sent Ella's thoughts into a tailspin.

Now by herself, she slumped onto the couch. Images of Benjamin clouded her thoughts—his strange eyes and the firm grip of his hands.

As Ella sat near the open window, a sudden breeze teased the curtains, bringing an unexpected chill to what had been a balmy evening. Yet, it wasn't the cool air that caught her breath, but an unseen, icy caress along her arm.

Then, as if called forth from the pages of her own thoughts, a colder, more distinct touch brushed across her face. In that moment, Ella realized Nathaniel was there before her, not a figment of her imagination, but as a ghost made manifest. His presence, ethereal yet real, brought not fear but a deep sense of peace, as if he were protecting her.

But as quickly as he appeared, Nathaniel's form faded and dissolved into the ether. Ella pondered the visitation in the silent room.

Later, as she settled into bed, Ella's mind drifted back to Benjamin. The events of the day, especially the unexpected side of Benjamin, replayed in her thoughts. It was a fleeting glimpse of something intense, a hint of vulnerability, contrasting with the familiar, comforting steadiness she knew. She wanted to clear the air between them, yet found her thoughts returning to Nathaniel.

The dream realm soon beckoned, drawing her into its mist-shrouded embrace. Nathaniel was there once more, his visage full of of pain and indignation. His attempt to speak, to bridge the silence that enveloped them, was futile.

His eyes clouded with hurt and a glint of anger that she did not understand, and his lips moved, trying to form words.

As their eyes met, a transformation occurred. The hardness in Nathaniel's expression gave way to a profound sadness, his demeanor softening as he reached out to Ella with a tenderness that spoke volumes. The ghostly tension that had flared between them dissolved, leaving only the gentle touch of his hands on her face, a touch that evoked memories of the Nathaniel she held dear in her heart. They stood there, locked in a silent embrace, and Ella felt a pang of longing so intense it was almost painful. She wished, more than ever, that he could be real, that she could hear his voice, feel his warmth, and be enveloped in the certainty of his love. But the dream, like all dreams, was fleeting, and as dawn approached, she felt him slip away, leaving her yearning for the next time they would meet in this realm.

CHAPTER SEVEN

A Dark Spirit Revealed

Ella steered her car through the tree-canopied streets, drawing closer to Benjamin's apartment. Her hands were firm on the steering wheel, the peculiar incident at her cottage still weighing on her mind. She hoped to find some clarity, or at least prove to herself she was just imagining things.

With every step closer to his door, Ella fought the urge to turn and flee. How would she even begin the conversation? Her knock was tentative, and a brief silence lingered before the door swung open, revealing Benjamin. His warm, inviting grin—so normal—melted away the uncertainty that had enveloped Ella.

"Ella," he greeted. "What a surprise."

She smiled. "I hope it's a good time?"

"Always," he assured, stepping aside.

His home was a sanctuary, steeped in history and mystery. An alcove in one corner was adorned with relics from yesteryear and towering stacks of books. Scattered across the desk, evidence of his recent endeavors lay in the clutter.

They sat on the couch not speaking, until Benjamin offered, "Tea? Coffee?"

"Coffee, please," Ella responded.

As Benjamin retreated to the kitchen, the gentle clink of cups and the shuffle of his movements provided a soothing backdrop to Ella's thoughts. The air filled with the rich, earthy aroma of coffee, drifting through the space and coaxing a sense of calm anticipation.

When he returned, Benjamin handed her a mug and looked at her. "To what do I owe this visit?"

Ella exhaled, clutching the mug for warmth and courage. "I've been replaying the events at my cottage... and I thought we should talk. Try to make sense of it all."

The atmosphere shifted. An eerie coldness spread through the room, making Ella's skin prickle with goosebumps. The comforting warmth seemed to dissipate almost instantly, and the curtains fluttered despite the closed windows. Meanwhile, a faint whisper seemed to dance at the edge of her hearing.

Benjamin's expression became serious. "What happened? I don't understand."

"The other day at my place."

The air in the room grew heavier as the temperature continued to drop. Benjamin's body seemed to stiffen, his posture altering. His relaxed demeanor vanished, replaced by a rigidity that was foreign to his nature. For a split second, his eyes glazed over before darkening to an almost black hue, losing their usual warmth.

His breathing slowed, every exhale more pronounced than the last, filling the room with tension. Ella watched with growing apprehension as his fingers tightened around his mug.

When he finally spoke, his voice was deeper, laced with a strange undertone. "You didn't like that? Your body said otherwise." The aggression in his words, so unlike the Benjamin she knew, sent an icy shiver down Ella's spine. It was as though something else, some darker force, had taken residence in him.

The room grew charged with a tension that Ella could almost touch. She hesitated, her thoughts racing as she tried to piece together the puzzle of Benjamin's behavior.

"I... I was taken aback. It wasn't the Benjamin I knew. It was...intense, so unlike you."

His eyes seemed distant. There was a fleeting glimmer of recognition of the kind-hearted man she knew, but it was clouded by darkness. "Are you scared of me now, Ella?"

Ella swallowed her fear. "No, I'm not scared. Just...worried. That wasn't you, Benjamin. The connection we share has always been genuine, deep. But that night... it felt... different..."

The shadow in Benjamin's eyes lifted, replaced by genuine confusion. "I...I don't understand it either. Ever since that night at the cottage, it's as if I'm being pulled in two directions. There's a force, a pressure that sometimes takes over."

Ella, despite her instincts screaming at her to run, leaned forward, her hand finding his. "That's what terrifies me. It wasn't just aggression. It felt... possessed, like you weren't in control."

His gaze flickered with defiance and fear. "What are you saying, Ella? That I'm haunted? That some spirit has control over me?"

She inhaled, steadying herself. "I don't know, but I can't deny what I felt, what I saw. Something changed in you, and it just happened again."

Benjamin's face crumpled, realization sinking in. "I... I never want to be a threat to you, Ella. If I ever scared you, I'm sorry. You should go."

Her eyes locked with his. "We're going to figure this out, okay? It's like our paths are caught up in... I don't know, some sort of history? There's something pulling us together. We've got to deal with it before it overwhelms us."

As her words hung in the air, a shift occurred in Benjamin again. It was as though the room had taken a breath. The warmth in Benjamin's apartment was gone. Comforting sounds of day now distant, muffled echoes, filtered through water. It was as if the surrounding space had contracted and the walls inched inward in a suffocating embrace.

Benjamin's voice cut through the silence, alien and dark. "Why so scared?" he murmured, his tone chilling, his smile a sinister smirk. "Don't you crave the closeness, the deep heart of our bond?"

Before Ella could react, Benjamin's aggression became physical, pushing her onto the couch with surprising speed. Despite the cushioning, the force left her breathless, feeling his icy presence against her warmth.

The change in his eyes unsettled her. This was not Benjamin. Her heart raced with a mix of confusion and fear.

She attempted to free herself, but his presence was overpowering, a stark reminder of the unexpected turn their encounter had taken.

"You can't ignore this," he whispered. His words left her feeling exposed.

Tears brimmed in Ella's eyes. She wanted to call out, but her voice seemed lost, choked by the knot of fear in her throat. Just when despair seemed to take hold, the room's energy shifted again.

The flickering lights waged a war against the encroaching darkness, while outside, the wind rose in a protective crescendo. A gust burst through the room, sending papers into a chaotic dance. A glowing figure emerged, standing as a beacon of hope.

It was Nathaniel.

The spirit glowed with a pale light. His eyes filled with determination and anguish. They were fixed on Benjamin. Without uttering a word, Nathaniel raised his arms, creating an impenetrable barrier that shielded Ella. The room crackled with electric tension as the two forces — one dark and menacing, the other protective and radiant — clashed.

Benjamin, or the entity controlling him, let out a guttural roar of frustration. "She is mine—they are all mine," the entity declared.

Nathaniel, unshaken, countered with a calm authority that filled the charged air. "She rests under my protection."

As the standoff continued, Ella, fueled by adrenaline and sheer willpower, broke free from the grip of fear. She made a beeline for the door, sparing one last glance at the scene playing out behind her.

Outside, the air wrapped around her, slicing through the terror that clouded her thoughts. She hurried to her car, the ground beneath her feet blurring as she moved. With her heart hammering against her ribs, she started the engine and sped away from Benjamin's apartment. Tears streamed down her face, not from fear, but also from the crushing realization that she had left Benjamin alone to deal with whatever that was.

As she arrived back home, the night's events pressing upon her and she collected her thoughts. Just then, her phone buzzed with a text from Benjamin: *Where did you go?*

Had to get home, she replied. At least she knew he was safe and unaware of the night's ordeal. Clearly, she was the catalyst for something inexplicable.

She knew she couldn't put this call off any longer.

Ashlyn Alden

Ella had been reluctant to make the call, yet desperation drove her to act. After a moment of clumsiness with her phone, she dialed the number, her breath held in suspense as it rang.

A breathy voice answered. "Hello, this is Ashlyn."

"Hello... My name is Ella," she began. "Benjamin Hartley gave me your number. I'm not sure if he mentioned me, but... I need your help."

A soft sigh came from the other end. "Ah, Ella. I was wondering when you'd call. Benjamin has spoken of you. What's happened?"

Ella recounted the evening's events, along with the other unsettling experiences she'd faced in recent times. She even mentioned her dreams, but not in much detail.

Ashlyn listened, pausing Ella to ask a question. "Ella, in these visions or dreams, do you feel you're watching or actively living them?"

"It feels... real. Like I'm there, experiencing everything," Ella admitted.

"And Benjamin's behavior, does it change suddenly or over time?"

"It's sudden, usually during emotional moments or when discussing these... incidents," Ella whispered.

Ashlyn was silent for a moment, processing. "Ella, more is going on than meets the eye. I believe you're caught in something much larger than you realize. And while I'm cautious about sharing others' personal matters, I think you should know I've been working with Benjamin, help-ing him understand certain... abilities."

Ella's brow furrowed in confusion. "Abilities?"

"It's not my place to go into details," Ashlyn replied. "However, it's fortunate timing that I'm in town for the paranormal investigation. How about we meet tomorrow at the museum on West Street? Does 11 work for you? There's something there I believe you should see."

Relief flooded Ella. "Thank you, Ashlyn. I'll be there tomorrow, at 11."

The call ended, and though Ella was filled with un-ease, she felt a spark of hope. Whatever was unfolding, she would not face it alone.

* * *

The world of dreams has a unique way of distorting time and space, making the unbelievable seem ordinary, and bringing the distant close. That night, as Ella's con-sciousness sank into the gentle embrace of sleep, she found herself again in the realm where the spectral and the living coalesced.

The familiar sound of waves crashing against rocks greeted her, and when she opened her eyes, she stood at the very peak of the Misthaven lighthouse. The ambiance was surreal. An otherworldly glow enveloped the space, bathing everything in a silvery light that seemed to emanate from the moon.

Standing before her was Nathaniel. He appeared more tangible than ever, his form no longer the fleeting, translucent apparition she'd grown accustomed to. The very air around him pulsed with energy, making the space between them feel charged.

They gravitated toward each other, the pull between them undeniable. As they came face to face, their fingers brushing, a rush of emotions surged through Ella. Memories, not her own sensations, feelings, and glimpses of a time long past, played out before her eyes.

The dream felt more like a journey through time than random images. Ella was adrift in a sea of memories, each wave crashing against the shore of her consciousness with the vividness of a lived moment. She was a little girl again, her laughter echoing against the sturdy walls of the lighthouse that had been her childhood sanctuary. The dream painted her younger self with a palette in hand, strokes of vibrant colors blending into forms and shapes on canvas.

The scene shifted, and there she was, looking up into her mother's eyes—eyes that sparkled with life and love, a memory untouched by the shadow of death. Her father's voice, a firm reprimand, cautioned her each time she spoke of the ghostly figures that only she could see.

Then, a younger Nathaniel appeared before her, his presence igniting a spark that illuminated her soul. It was love at first sight, a moment of profound connection that defied words, as if their souls recognized each other from lifetimes past.

As the dream wove these memories together, the distinction between observer and participant blurred. At first, Ella watched these moments unfold as if she were a spectator in her own life, but the dream enveloped her. The barrier between herself and the young girl in the memory dissipating until they became the same.

She questioned the origins of these memories. Were they hers, or did they belong to Isabella? The dream shifted between past and present, weaving Ella's emotions and experiences with those of a life that might once have been hers, leaving her to wonder at the interconnection of souls and the timeless nature of love and loss.

As dawn's early light made itself known, a shift occurred to Nathaniel. His playful tenderness was replaced by an urgency that gripped Ella's attention. He tried to communicate, his eyes darting with distress and a desperate need to convey something vital. With every attempt to speak, his voice seemed choked, stifled by an unseen force.

Nathaniel didn't need words to convey his warning. His anxious demeanor spoke volumes. Ella's mind was awash with unsettling images. Cautionary flashes appeared in front of her and the dark outline of a spirit seemed to seethe with rage. Nathaniel's message was crystal clear—beware of the angry ghost lurking ahead.

The fabric of their shared dream unraveled, drawing them back towards the stark light of reality. Nathaniel's figure stretched out, a desperate attempt to bridge the growing gap between them. In a silent whisper, he mouthed a name: "Isabella." The echo of that name lingered, a presence in the room, unveiling the painful truth that perhaps Ella wasn't the focus of his desires, but a shadow of his long-lost love.

Now fully awakened, Ella's heart ached with emotions—the beauty of their dream entangled with the sharpness of Nathaniel's whisper. Caught in a whirlwind of feelings, she navigated the blurred lines where past dreams and present realities converge.

Ella pulled her knees to her chest, wrapping her arms around them for comfort. She felt alone. Nathaniel's heart belonged to someone else, and Benjamin was under the control of something evil. The thought left her adrift.

She held onto the hope that her meeting with Ashlyn tomorrow might shed some light on these dark circumstances. Answers were what she needed, and perhaps Ashlyn could provide them. It was a slim hope, but it was all she had to cling to during her confusion and fear.

CHAPTER EIGHT

A Twist in the Tale

In the halls of the local museum, the air was thick with anticipation. The sleepy coastal town buzzed with whispers, its heartbeat quickened by the promise of recognition from the upcoming episode of the ghost hunter show. The town council, in a stroke of inspiration, had seized upon this opportunity, curating a new exhibit that delved into the area's haunted legacy. It was a clever ruse, designed to entice tourists and ghost enthusiasts alike to their quiet shores.

Ella wandered among the exhibits, reading the captions and taking it all in. Each display was a portal to the past, arranged with relics that whispered of forgotten lives. She could see Benjamin's hand in some displays and wondered if he had worked on them. There were diaries frayed at the edges, photographs faded with time, and objects that once held meaning in the hands of their original owners.

The lighting in the room was a deliberate choice, casting a warm, amber glow that seemed to pull the shadows back just enough to illuminate the treasures of yesteryear. Around her, the murmurs of other visitors floated, full of excitement and speculation about the ghost hunter show and the secrets it promised to unveil.

Drawn as if by a magnet, Ella stood before a display that called to her very soul. It featured Misthaven Light. Among the artifacts, a photograph captured her gaze and held it fast. It depicted two men, standing side by side with an air of camaraderie and solemn duty. One figure was Nathaniel, and the man beside him bore a striking resemblance to someone she knew all too well—Benjamin.

The shock of the recognition rooted her to the spot, her thoughts raced as she absorbed the revelation. The elegant script on the caption of the date etching itself into her memory: "Lighthouse Keeper Nathaniel and friend, Samuel Hartley, 1879" A surge of unease washed over her. Benjamin had never mentioned that Samuel's surname was Hartley, too—and now this. Samuel looked JUST like Benjamin. The resemblance was unsettling.

Implications of the photograph spiraled through her mind, intertwining with the hauntings and Benjamin's strange behavior. Was it Samuel that possessed him? It was as if the past refused to remain silent, each piece of the puzzle falling into place with an almost audible click. Ella knew that the mysteries of the lighthouse—and the connections between Nathaniel, Isabella, and now Samuel and Benjamin,—were far from resolved.

As she stood there, a deeper discomfort settled, stemming from how much she herself looked like Isabella. What if Samuel had been Isabella's killer? Was history fated to repeat itself, casting her and Benjamin in their tragic roles? This personal connection to the lore felt too close, making her skin crawl.

The secrets buried in the town's history were dragging her deeper into a story she had not expected. Despite the discomfort and the growing fear, Ella felt an irresistible pull towards uncovering these hidden truths. The past, with its ghostly whispers and unresolved mysteries, beckoned, and she found herself powerless to resist its call.

A hushed voice behind her remarked, "Ah, you've noticed Samuel, haven't you?"

Startled, Ella whirled around to find herself face-to-face with a captivating woman. Raven-black hair flowed down her back, framing pale blue eyes that sparkled with an otherworldly intensity—it was Ashlyn Alden. Dressed in flowing garments, with a crystal pendant adorning her neck, every detail of her appearance whispered of her deep ties to the mystical.

"Benjamin bears a striking resemblance to Samuel Hartley, his ancestor," Ashlyn continued, and extended a graceful hand towards a secluded bench. "Shall we?" she suggested.

As they headed toward the spot, their path took them past displays rich with the lighthouse lore.

"It's quite the collection, isn't it?" Ashlyn remarked.

"It is," Ella agreed, her gaze stopping on an old logbook. "Every piece seems to hold a story eager to leap off the page—or out of the shadows."

After reaching the bench, the two introduced themselves, the initial unfamiliarity melting away as they exchanged names and smiles. "I'm Ashlyn Alden," said the woman, her handshake firm yet inviting.

"Ella Hayes," Ella responded.

After the initial pleasantries and a mutual recognition that they were on the cusp of exploring the extraordinary, Ashlyn leaned closer. With a low voice, she confided, "Since starting the lighthouse project, Benjamin has been tormented by dreams. These dreams connect him with Samuel and Nathaniel, suggesting the past is trying to tell us something. Given Benjamin's undeveloped psychic potential, he's unusually open to these messages."

Ella paused, a hint of color rising to her cheeks. "These dreams... are they intimate?" she asked.

As she observed Ella with a lifted eyebrow, Ashlyn replied in a measured tone, "Those dreams are Benjamin's to disclose, should he wish to." Her response, diplomatic yet firm, hinted at the depth of Benjamin's experiences, leaving Ella to ponder his psychic connection.

Feeling somewhat rebuffed, Ella attempted to redirect the conversation, her curiosity pushing her forward. "What do you know about these people historically, beyond mere photographs and legends?"

Ashlyn delved into the historical records she had come across, most of which Ella and Benjamin had already discussed. "There was a woman named Isabella Blackwell, a close friend to Samuel and engaged to Nathaniel. Tragically, her life was cut short, and the circumstances of her death were controversial. Both Nathaniel and Samuel were charged with her murder. While Nathaniel's alibi held — he was aboard a ship, far out at sea — Samuel's exoneration was largely attributed to his family's significant wealth and influence. The newspapers and gossip of the time believed Samuel's guilt, suggesting he might have taken drastic steps because of his unreciprocated feelings for Isabella."

"The Hartley family's wealth was legendary in the town, with roots that stretched back several generations. Originally making their fortune in shipping and trade, the Hartleys expanded their empire into various other ventures, ensuring that their coffers never ran dry. "

Ella's brows knitted in thought. "But that's just what people believed, isn't it? What do *you* see?" she couldn't help but probe deeper, seeking clarity from someone who could see beyond the veil of time.

Ashlyn took a moment, closing her eyes as if reaching into her psychic memories. "The impressions I've received are fluid and elusive. From what I've gathered, the relationship between Isabella and Samuel was one of genuine friendship. Pure, without romantic entanglement." She paused, her voice dropping a tad lower. "But Samuel... he had a different affection, one not for Isabella, but for Nathaniel. A love that was taboo in their era. It wasn't reciprocated, which might have been a source of pain for Samuel."

Ella's eyes widened in realization. "So the idea Samuel might have harmed Isabella out of jealousy could have been misconstrued?"

Ashlyn nodded. "At least in the way they suspected. But emotions, especially those suppressed and hidden, have a way of influencing events in ways we might not expect. We may never know what happened."

This revelation weighed on Ella. The interconnected lives of Isabella, Samuel, Nathaniel, and now, she and Benjamin, formed a web of history and emotion that was hard to disentangle. She felt sympathy for Samuel and a growing unease about the unresolved past that might haunt her present.

"It's important for me to know the specifics of the dreams you've had." Ashlyn's eyes met Ella's. "It might help us understand the connection better. Can you share them?"

Ella blushed, her fingers fidgeting with the hem of her shirt. "They're so... personal. Most of the time, it feels like it's just me and Nathaniel. We share these moments where emotions run so deep. But in the most recent dream, Nathaniel called me 'Isabella'. And that's when it hit me. Those feelings... they aren't really for me."

Ashlyns's brows furrowed. "That makes sense. You're channeling Isabella's memories, her emotions, her past. The bond you're feeling with Nathaniel in the dreams, it's the remnants of what Isabella felt for him."

"They started when I was on the other side of the country. How does that even work?" Ella took a shaky breath. "I didn't even know Misthaven Light existed."

"You may have your own latent abilities." Ashlyn pondered for a moment, the soft glow of the exhibit lighting casting shadows across her face. "Having an ancestor as a past life is quite rare, but it's not unheard of. It opens a unique channel for spiritual and emotional connections that can transcend time and space."

Ella nodded, absorbing Ashlyn's words. "Isabella isn't an ancestor, at least not that I'm aware of," she confessed. "But I suppose she could be. Without something like a DNA test, there's no way to know for sure." She sighed. "And really, whether she is or isn't doesn't change what's happening. This... connection, it's real, regardless of the reason."

Ashlyn leaned forward. "When exactly did you start having these dreams about Nathaniel?"

Ella thought back, trying to pinpoint the exact moment her nights became haunted by the past. "They started around late spring," she pursed her lips. "But I was on the other side of the country, which makes it even more bizarre. How does that even work?"

"That was around the time we first hired Benjamin to dig up history." Ashlyn nodded, a knowing look in her eyes. "It's clear that something has been stirred up. The timing of your dreams with Benjamin's research isn't a coincidence. It's as if the past is reaching out, using both of you as conduits to reconcile unfinished business."

Ella felt a chill run down her spine. The connection between her dreams and Benjamin's work was undeniable, and the thought that they might be part of something much larger than themselves was a bit terrifying, but also exhilarating.

"Am I safe?" Ella whispered.

Ashlyn leaned in, her tone taking on a more urgent note. "Benjamin confided in me he's been experiencing blackouts, moments when he doesn't remember his actions or what he's said. And sometimes, his personality... changes. It's unlike the Samuel I've seen in my impressions. Samuel's spirit is conflicted, but not malevolent. It's confusing and, frankly, I don't like being confused."

Ella's eyes widened in shock. "Why didn't he tell me?"

"He's terrified," Ashlyn responded. "And from my understanding, it seems Samuel's spirit is struggling within him."

Ella looked down at her hands and whispered, "I felt it, something dark and intense. But I also felt Benjamin, the real him, struggling beneath."

Ashlyn reached out, touching Ella's hand. "You're both caught in this drama from the past. And Ella," her voice dropped, "I *do* believe you have a latent psychic ability, too. You need to be careful."

Ella hesitated for a moment. "With all this happening, should Benjamin and I even go to Misthaven? Is it safe?"

"Under normal circumstances, I'd advise against it. However," Ashlyn sighed, "the connection you and Benjamin have with these spirits is undeniable. They won't let go until there's a resolution. And frankly, I believe the only way to uncover the truth and bring peace to these souls is to have both of you present on the island."

Ella's face drained of color. Ashlyns's words had hit her hard. "But that means..."

"Yes," Ashlyn interrupted, "it will be dangerous. You'll be diving into uncharted territories, confronting memories and emotions that have been suppressed for over a century."

Ashlyn's phone buzzed, breaking the intense atmosphere. She glanced at the message and sighed. "I need to meet with the show's team." She stood up, her flowing skirt rustling.

Ella hesitated for a moment, a trace of concern flickering in her eyes. "Ashlyn, do you think it's safe for me to be around Benjamin right now?" she asked, the question hanging in the air between them.

Ashlyn paused, considering Ella's question. "Given everything that's happening, it might be wise to keep your interactions in public places for the time being," she advised. "Until I have time to meet with the two of you together, we can't be too cautious. The energies at play here are complex, and we need to understand them better before we can make any definitive judgments about safety."

Ella nodded, reassurance washing over her despite the uncertainty of the situation. "Okay, I can do that. It's just... all of this is so overwhelming. I never imagined anything like this could happen."

"We will talk more, and I will make sure you are prepared. Trust your instincts. You'll get through this," Ashlyn reassured her, offering a comforting smile.

Ella managed a small smile in return. "Take care. We'll be in touch," she said, her voice steadier than before.

As Ashlyn's figure melded with the crowd and vanished from sight, the burden of their exchanged words settled upon Ella's shoulders. Caught in history, emotions, and otherworldly happenings, the true depth of their entanglement with spirits long gone was clear. The realization was overwhelming, casting a shadow over her understanding of the present and its ties to the past.

Ella inhaled, the cool air of the museum grounding her. She wandered through the remaining displays, trying to process everything. There were so many layers to unravel, so many truths hidden in the folds of time. The most pressing matter was Benjamin. Their experiences, his blackouts, the dreams — everything was intertwined. And the realization that he was vulnerable too only heightened her concern.

Her fingers hovered over her phone, hesitating for a moment. With a sigh, she dialed Benjamin's number. It rang twice before he picked up.

"Ella?" His voice was soft.

"Benjamin," she began, searching for the right words. "We need to talk."

There was a pause, and she could imagine him nodding on the other end. "Come over. We can—"

"No," she interrupted. Ashlyn had advised public places. "I'd feel better if we were somewhere public."

She could hear the hurt in his sigh. "Alright. How about the coffee shop? The one where we first met?"

Ella nodded, even though he couldn't see her. "That sounds perfect."

"Okay, see you there," he murmured, and with that, the call ended.

The bell above the door tinkled as Ella entered The Harbor Brew. The familiar scent of roasted coffee beans enveloped her, offering comfort. It was a setting she cherished, with the gentle hum of whispered conversations and the soft lighting lending a soothing aura. Their corner, with its worn-out leather seats, was occupied by Benjamin, who looked up when she approached.

His expression was a muddle of worry and relief when she mentioned Ashlyn. "You met with her?"

Ella nodded, settling across from him. "Yes, and before you get too worried, she didn't tell me any personal secrets you shared with her." She offered him a reassuring smile, though she could sense the tension radiating from him. "She respects privacy."

Benjamin ran a hand through his hair, looking relieved. "Thank you for telling me."

"Which brings me to my next point," she said. "We can't have secrets between us anymore. Not with everything that's going on."

He hesitated, eyes darting away from hers. He knew what she was talking about. "I found out about Samuel early in the research. The history, the tales... they all seemed to vilify him. They said he was responsible for Isabella's death. When I saw you for the first time and noticed the resemblance to her, I was afraid how you'd react. Especially because the moment our paths crossed, it felt like fate. It felt as if our souls had known each other forever."

Silence hung in the airt. "You recognized me when we met?" Ella asked, surprised.

"From the very instant," he admitted. "It felt like destiny. I just... didn't want history to cloud the present."

She let out a deep sigh. "We need transparency, Benjamin, especially now. We have to face it." She leaned forward, her voice soft. "Tell me about your dreams."

His face flushed a deep shade of crimson, his eyes darting around as if looking for an escape. "I... I don't really think that's necessary. It's embarrassing."

"Remember what we agreed," Ella insisted, her gaze unwavering. "No secrets."

After taking a shaky breath, he began, "Fine. My dreams... they're not about my love for Isabella. They're about Captain Nathaniel." He paused, looking down at the table. "I dream about... desires for Nathaniel."

Ella's eyes widened, taken aback. "As in...?"

Benjamin's face turned even redder, the tips of his ears burning. "Yes. Intimate desires. I'm not gay. At least I never thought I was, but the feelings are so real. So intense. It's confusing."

Their voices had become whispers now, their conversation too intimate for the casual ear to hear.

Ella hesitated, jealousy in her voice. "Did Nathaniel return his affections?"

Benjamin shook his head, looking almost relieved to confirm Nathaniel's indifference. "No. Not in any of those dreams. But..."

Benjamin's eyes shifted away, uncomfortable. "But sometimes Nathaniel seemed to... blend into my regular dreams. And in those moments, there was also... you."

Ella's heart rate quickened. She could feel a warmth creeping up her cheeks, but she tried to keep her voice casual. "Me? As in Ella or...?"

"As Isabella at first," he clarified, his voice quiet. "And sometimes as... well, just you."

She recognized her own dreams in his words. "I had similar dreams, where I wasn't sure if I was myself or Isabella. But Nathaniel... he seemed very real, very present."

Benjamin looked at her with raised eyebrows. "What do you mean?"

She hesitated, her fingers playing with the rim of her coffee mug. "It's... it's hard to explain. Sometimes it felt like he was... reaching out to me, calling me."

Benjamin leaned forward, his voice gentle yet insistent. "Ella, you need to tell me everything, too."

She bit her lip, looking away. "I don't know if I can. It's just too personal."

He reached out, placing a hand over hers. "Remember, communication is a two-way street. You wanted transparency from me. I need the same from you."

Ella's fingers played with the necklace she was wearing. "In these dreams, it was often sunset at the lighthouse. The sky is painted in hues of orange and pink, the horizon a blend of the sea and the skies. Nathaniel would stand there, in his captain's uniform, looking out at the sea. And then, he'd turn to me... to Isabella, I mean, and there was always this deep longing in his eyes."

She paused, gathering her thoughts. "It wasn't just the surroundings, Benjamin. It was the emotions. They were so real. Sometimes he'd reach out, holding me close, and other times we would just stand side by side, lost in our own world. There was love there, a deep connection. But it was also tinged with sadness like there was always something unsaid between them."

Benjamin's jaw tightened as he listened, his fingers drumming on the table. There was a shadow in his eyes, one that spoke of jealousy and confusion, but he remained silent, letting Ella continue.

She sighed, "Sometimes the dreams got more—intimate."

As she gazed into Benjamin's eyes, she ventured further, "But it wasn't just about embodying Isabella's emotions. I felt them as my own. The depth of feeling, the bond, the yearning—it all seemed so tangible, as though Nathaniel and I shared a past."

An uneasy silence enveloped them. Benjamin's expression remained unreadable, yet the tightness in his posture betrayed his discomfort. "It's a lot to take in, Ella," he confessed, his voice strained. "The idea of you—or Isabella—experiencing such intense connections, even in dreams... I almost feel jealous," he blushed.

Ella scanned their surroundings in the quaint coffee shop, ensuring their conversation remained private. The space around them felt cocooned, the soft murmur of patrons and the clinking of cups forming a serene backdrop.

"Could you share more about your dreams?" She asked as she leaned in.

Benjamin let out a sigh, his eyes flickering with hesitation before he spoke. "In one particular dream, which felt more like Samuel's wishes than actual events, we were in this small room, the ambiance heavy with anticipation. Samuel—I mean, I was there with Nathaniel, and the air was thick with unspoken tension."

He paused, collecting his thoughts. "There was a moment of hesitation, a look that conveyed so much without words. And suddenly, the distance between us vanished."

Carefully choosing his words, he continued, "It was a dream of seeking and finding comfort in each other's presence, a gentle, almost hesitant connection. We were navigating the complexities of our feelings, trying to understand them."

Ella, intrigued by the vulnerability in his admission, encouraged him, "It sounds like an experience."

"It was," Benjamin admitted, the complexity of his emotions clear. "It left me questioning and reflecting. I've experienced nothing like it."

Ella nodded. "I can imagine. It's all so interconnected, isn't it? Our dreams, the past... I think Ashlyn's insights could help us untangle some of this."

Benjamin looked thoughtful, his earlier tension easing. "I hope so. She seems to have a good understanding of these matters."

Ella leaned forward, her eyes sparkling. "I'm excited about the investigation. Not just for answers, but to see how all of this…," she gestured, encompassing their discussions, the dreams, and the psychic's guidance, "…fits together."

"Me too," Benjamin agreed. "And I'm glad we're doing this together. Whatever happens, it feels like we're on the right path to understanding the bigger picture."

Ella smiled.. "Exactly. And who knows? Maybe this will bring some closure to the spirits involved, too."

"Agreed." He chuckled.

As the conversation dwindled, a comfortable silence settled between Ella and Benjamin. They found the world around them fading into the background. It was one of those rare moments where words were unnecessary, where the connection between two people spoke volumes more than conversation ever could. Just as they were about to lean closer, a sudden buzz shattered the moment. Their phones vibrated in unison, pulling them back from the moment. With a shared smile, they reached for their devices.

It was a message from Ashlyn. *Investigation is on for tomorrow. Can we meet before boarding the boat? There are some things we need to go over.*

Let's meet at my place, Ella texted back, Benjamin nodding in approval as he peered over her shoulder.

See you both in the morning. Stay safe tonight. Ashlyn's last text read, a reminder of the seriousness beneath their excitement.

With a shared grin, they acknowledged the adventure that lay ahead.

"See you in the morning for the big reveal," Benjamin said.

"Can't wait," she responded, her voice full of resolve.

Then, with a promise of tomorrow's mysteries hanging in the air, they went their separate ways.

CHAPTER NINE

Between Two Worlds

Ashlyn arrived first, enveloped in the wave of mystery and otherworldliness that always seemed to swirl around her. Ella welcomed her at the door with a warm smile. "Coffee, tea?" she offered, leading her guest into the cozy kitchen.

"Tea, please," Ashlyn replied, her voice soft yet clear.

Ella busied herself with the tea, placing two mugs on the table before sitting down opposite Ashlyn. The atmosphere was filled with an anticipatory silence, the kind that precedes a storm of revelations.

"I wanted to get here early to prepare you for what I fear is unfolding with Benjamin," Ashlyn began, her gaze fixed on Ella with an intensity that felt almost palpable. "And perhaps to help you understand yourself better."

"I appreciate it," Ella replied. "I believe he's a good person, but the things happening have been quite frightening."

Ashlyn nodded, understanding the depth of Ella's concern. "My psychic abilities are strongest in the realm of retro cognition. I receive glimpses of events that have already happened, sometimes triggered by people, but most often by places with intense energy. Venturing to Misthaven Island will give me a clearer picture of what transpired. However, my visions are more akin to memories, colored by the emotions and perceptions of those who experienced them firsthand. In the end, it may be that one had to be there to grasp the full truth."

She continued, her voice gaining a note of passion as she spoke of her work with paranormal investigation groups. "Knowing the history, coupled with the emotions and perceptions surrounding a haunting, increases the likelihood of gathering tangible evidence—and yes, it makes for a good show. Some groups are committed to understanding the phenomena, while for others, it's more about the viewership."

"And where do you stand in all this?" Ella asked, curiosity piqued by Ashlyn's dedication.

Ashlyn laughed, a sound that seemed to echo around the room. "If I didn't need to eat, I'd do it for free. There's nothing more fulfilling than helping a kindred spirit, whether in life or death! The connection, the moment of understanding and peace it can bring, is unparalleled. It's not just about the thrill of the investigation or the chase for evidence. It's about providing closure, answers, and sometimes, just the comfort of knowing one isn't alone in their experiences."

Ella listened, captivated by Ashlyn's words and the earnestness in her eyes. Ashlyn was driven by a deep-seated desire to aid both the living and the dead, a mission that went far beyond mere curiosity or the lure of the mysterious. In this moment, Ella felt hopeful, a sense that perhaps, with Ashlyn's help, they could unravel the mysteries that had been plaguing them and, in doing so, find a path to peace and understanding.

"So, where do Benjamin and I fit into all of this?" Ella asked, her brows furrowed in a mixture of concern and curiosity. Ashlyn's lips curved into a knowing, almost secretive smile.

"The force is strong in you," she quipped, her laughter lightening the moment with her playful reference. Seeing Ella's expectant look, she became serious again. "Honestly, it's rare to encounter two individuals so deeply intertwined with a haunting. And you, Ella, drawn all the way from the other side of the country—it's as if the spirits themselves are clamoring for someone to unravel this mystery!"

Ella nodded, her mind racing with thoughts and possibilities. "Do you think Samuel was responsible? Do you believe he pushed Isabella?"

Ashlyn exhaled, her expression clouding over. "I can't say for certain. My visions only offer glimpses, fragments of the past. Samuel's presence is there, but the energies surrounding that moment are so muddled, so conflicting. It's as though he was battling within himself, possibly suffering from some kind of identity disorder. Yet, diagnosing a living person with such a condition is challenging enough in modern times, let alone speculating on the complex emotions of a spirit long passed."

Ella let out a soft sigh, her thoughts drifting to Benjamin. She was fond of him, but the idea of being close to someone mixed up with a dangerous spirit was daunting. "And Benjamin?" she asked, her voice barely above a whisper. "Do you think he'll be okay?"

Ashlyn's smile returned, this time imbued with a warmth and reassurance that touched Ella. "I believe so. I sense that once we reach the island and explore the actual scene of the haunting, I'll be able to help free him from his spectral stowaway."

Their intense discussion was interrupted by two soft raps at the door. Benjamin had arrived.

The sudden intrusion jolted Ella back to the present, her heart skipping a beat at the thought of facing Benjamin now, with all these swirling questions and fears. Yet Ashlyn's confident, reassuring presence gave her a glimmer of hope. Perhaps, together, they could confront the mysteries of the past and help Benjamin find peace.

As she rose to answer the door, Ella took a moment to steady her nerves, preparing herself for the uncertain journey ahead. The path to solving the mystery of the haunting, and understanding the roles they each played in it, was bound to be fraught with challenges. Yet, the prospect of uncovering the truth, and perhaps in doing so, bringing peace to restless spirits, filled her with a sense of purpose she hadn't realized she'd been seeking.

Benjamin's bright eyes sparked a flutter of butterflies in Ella's stomach—the good kind—as she welcomed him inside. "Hi," she greeted, her voice a soft whisper in the cozy room. "Do you want some coffee?"

He nodded, his gaze filled with a warmth that hinted at a longing for closeness, yet he hesitated as if unsure of the boundaries between them. "It's okay," she reassured him with a gentle smile, leaning in to give him a comforting hug. "I think we're safe here," she added, her laughter tinged with a nervous edge that betrayed her calm exterior.

As they gathered around the kitchen table, Ashlyn wasted no time diving into the heart of the matter. "I wanted to meet with you both first because I believe there's some heavy stuff entwined with this investigation. The crew and the other investigators are going to be all business, focusing more on capturing good shots and building a TV show than on the spirits' feelings. But from what I sense around you two, the impact of this investigation is going to hit you like a ton of bricks! You'll need to establish spiritual boundaries, or it could overwhelm you."

"How do we do that?" Benjamin asked. As a history student, the idea of history reaching out to communicate with him had left him unnerved.

Ashlyn offered a reassuring smile. "Think of yourself as a doctor or therapist. You need to set clear parameters with the spirits—define your 'office hours' and establish where these interactions can take place. Being on the island will present its challenges, but it also offers the best opportunity to set these limits. You can tell the spirits that you've come to their territory to engage with them, but they need to respect your boundaries. No more hitching a ride in your mind," she directed at Benjamin, then turning her attention to Ella, she added, "or in your dreams." Her gaze shifted back to Benjamin, seeking his understanding.

"Understood," Benjamin replied, a faint blush coloring his cheeks, showing his apprehension yet willingness to proceed.

Ella watched the exchange, a sense of solidarity building between them. Ashlyn's guidance provided a practical approach to navigating the uncharted waters of their investigation, offering a semblance of control over interactions that, until now, seemed beyond their grasp. Setting boundaries with the spirits, of treating their interactions as structured meetings, was comforting. It gave Ella and Benjamin a framework to protect themselves while delving into the mysteries that awaited them on the island.

Ashlyn outlined the plan, ensuring Ella and Benjamin understood each step. "We'll meet the crew at the docks," she began, her voice carrying a note of excitement. "The boat will take us to Misthaven Island, all above board with permission from the state. We'll all head over together."

"Once on the island," Ashlyn continued, "the camera crew will set up, taking advantage of the remaining daylight to capture shots of the island's scenic beauty. Benjamin, you'll be up first. As our historian, you'll be filmed detailing the history of the island and sharing the facts we know about its previous inhabitants—all the material you've already prepared."

Then, turning her attention to Ella, Ashlyn added with a wink, "There won't be much for you to do in that capacity, so you might find yourself taking on a variety of tasks. Most of the time, they don't bring along a historian's 'assistant,'" she teased, "so the director will probably put you to work wherever needed."

Ella and Benjamin absorbed the information, nodding along. Ella felt a surge of excitement. The anticipation was building, transforming her nerves into a buzzing excitement.

As they journeyed to the dock, Benjamin's car was enveloped in a contemplative silence, each passenger immersed in personal reflections. Sunshine bathed the day, casting a hopeful glow on their expedition. Upon arrival, they were greeted by the bustling crew, busy loading equipment. The atmosphere was serene, resembling a group gearing up for an afternoon cruise more than a team on the brink of unraveling the mysteries of a haunted island.

They watched the crew work. The professional manner in which they handled the gear and coordinated their efforts offered a reassuring glimpse into the forthcoming investigation's seriousness. Yet, the beautiful weather and the gentle lapping of the water against the dock lent an air of calm to the proceedings.

This was something significant, a chance to delve into the past and explore the untold stories of Misthaven Island. With Ashlyn's guidance, Benjamin's historical knowledge, and her own willingness to take on whatever role was needed, Ella was ready to face whatever the island had in store for them. The adventure was about to begin, and she couldn't wait to set sail into the unknown.

The salty sea breeze tousled Ella's hair as the motorboat bobbed on the waves. Misthaven Light, with its distinctive square tower piercing through the keeper's house, stood on the horizon.

Beside her, Benjamin leaned in, his warm breath mingling with the cool sea air. "It's even more mesmerizing up close, isn't it?" His voice held a note of wonder, his eyes reflecting the shimmering water.

Ella nodded, lost in the moment. "There's a sense of timelessness to it. Like it's been waiting just for us." Her fingers brushed against his, sending tingling currents up her arm.

Ashlyn, positioned at the front, shouted over the wind's hum. "This place holds many secrets. I feel them even now. It's eager to share its tales." She looked back at Ella and Benjamin, her piercing eyes softened. "And you two—be mindful of the living and the dead. This island can be quite... enchanting."

The boat's gentle sway, combined with the rhythmic lullaby of the lapping waves, brought them closer. Their shoulders touched, their shared anticipation building a bridge of intimacy. "Nervous?" Ella asked, her voice almost a whisper.

"A bit," Benjamin admitted, his fingers tracing hers. "But more excited. There's so much history here, and then there's... us."

The boat docked, its wooden planks creaking underfoot. As the team prepared for the shoot, the world seemed to pause, allowing Ella and Benjamin a moment suspended in time, the past and present intertwined under the watchful gaze of the lighthouse.

The team had a well-rehearsed rhythm, transitioning from the boat ride to preparing for the day's shoot and night's investigation. Their show, having aired multiple seasons, had garnered a loyal following. The blend of history, technology, and psychic insights made it a unique addition to the paranormal community.

Martin, the lead investigator, was tall and broad-shouldered. His dark hair was neatly combed, and a pair of round glasses perched on his nose gave him an academic appearance. Beside him was Travis, shorter but with an athletic build, exuding a quiet confidence. They had been friends long before the show's inception and their bond showed in the way they communicated—often without words.

While the duo conferred on the night's strategy, two camera operators, Naomi, a petite woman with pixie-cut blonde hair, and Raul, a burly man with a kind face, started setting up tripods and adjusting their lens angles. Lydia, the sound expert, tested her audio equipment, ensuring that every whisper, every EVP, would be captured.

Ashlyn, sensing Ella's curiosity, gestured at the infrared cameras being set up near the base of the lighthouse. "Those will help us see in the dark, and sometimes, they pick up figures or anomalies that the naked eye misses."

Ella, eyes wide, responded, "It's so fascinating. Do you need any help?"

Travis, overhearing, smiled. "Thanks for the offer, Ella, but we've got a system. Too many hands can sometimes make things tricky. But ask questions, and if you feel or see anything off, let us know."

Benjamin, already conversing with Martin about the island's history, nodded in agreement. "We're here to observe and assist when needed. Let the professionals do their job."

Once everything was set up, it was time for Benjamin to film the historical information.

Ella stood a little apart from the crew, her gaze fixed on Benjamin Hartley as he prepared to delve into the history of Misthaven Light. There was an air of earnest anticipation about her, her eyes betraying something deeper, something personal whenever they rested on Benjamin. The rustic backdrop of the lighthouse added a layer of intrigue to the scene, almost as if it were a silent character in their unfolding story.

As Benjamin began speaking, Ella couldn't help but admire the way his voice danced with excitement. "Early photographs of Misthaven Light reveal a basic square shape," he said, his scholarly enthusiasm infectious. Ella imagined the lighthouse as he described it: a unique, twelve-foot square brick tower emerging from a flat-roofed keeper's dwelling, its metal stairs mimicking the building's square form.

Her attention drifted as Martin interrupted Benjamin, asking him to emphasize the uniqueness of the structure. Ella smiled. She appreciated Benjamin's willingness to adapt, to make his wealth of knowledge accessible and engaging.

Benjamin cleared his throat and restarted, his voice now infused with a touch more drama. Ella found herself drawn in by his vivid storytelling, hanging on to every word about the lighthouse's construction and the early tragedies that befell the keeper's family.

When Benjamin described the ferocious gale of 1856, Ella could almost hear the howling winds and crashing waves, see the sea surging over the rock, sweeping away the fuel shed. His ability to bring history to life always amazed her, and today was no exception.

When Benjamin delved into the lighthouse's history, he spoke of the disturbing discovery made during its construction. "In 1854, as the foundation was being laid, workers unearthed human remains, an unsettling omen that delayed the project. Some say it was the body of a local captain, Elias Thorton, who had been lost to the sea," he revealed. Ella felt a shiver at the thought. The nature of these remains, shrouded in mystery, had been the subject of much speculation over the years.

He then recounted the tragedies that befell the lighthouse's first keeper, Armand Blackwood, and his family. "Armand's tenure was marked by sorrow from the outset. His infant son, born just a few weeks after they moved in, succumbed to unknown ailments, a devastating start to their life here." Ella felt a twinge of sadness, imagining the family's initial joy turning to mourning.

"The grief continued," Benjamin continued, "when Clara, Armand's wife, passed away in 1862, succumbing to a swift and merciless illness." His voice carried a note of sympathy that resonated with Ella. She pictured Clara, a figure of resilience turned frail by her untimely death.

Benjamin's narrative then took a darker turn as he spoke of Isabella's tragic end in 1875. "Isabella, their beloved daughter, met a tragic fate at just 19. She fell from the cliffs, her body claimed by the churning waters below." The sorrow in his tone was palpable, and Ella felt the family's tragedies as if they were her own.

"The death of Isabella broke Armand," Benjamin said. "He passed away a year later in 1876, some say of a broken heart, while others whispered of guilt. His death, like his daughter's, was shrouded in mystery and unresolved sorrow."

He then moved on to Nathaniel Hawthorn, Isabella's betrothed, and the next keeper. "Nathaniel, overcome by grief at the loss of his love, became a recluse, his life at the lighthouse marked by solitude until his untimely death in 1885, under circumstances that remain as mysterious as the island itself."

As Benjamin concluded, weaving together the threads of the lighthouse's history with the mystery of the curse, Ella felt a surge of admiration for him. His words hung in the air, a poignant reminder of the mysteries they were there to uncover.

The camera zoomed out, capturing the haunting beauty of the lighthouse against the darkening sky. Ella's thoughts lingered on Benjamin. His passion for history, his ability to animate the past, and the subtle warmth in his voice—all these qualities deepened the affection she felt for him.

Ella approached Benjamin as the crew took a brief respite, their equipment still poised for the night's paranormal investigation. The dying light of the day cast long shadows around Misthaven Light, adding an air of anticipation for the evening's activities.

"Benjamin," she said. "Your presentation was fantastic. You have a way of making the past come alive."

He turned toward her and blushed. "Thanks. I was nervous. I'm used to doing lectures for a bunch of stoic historians. I think these viewers are different."

His words hung in the air between them, mingling with the growing sense of mystery as the sky darkened. Around them, the crew was enjoying a well-deserved break, their laughter and chatter a contrast to the eerie quiet that surrounded the lighthouse.

"Speaking of tonight," Benjamin continued, lowering his voice to a whisper, "are you nervous? Think we'll encounter the ghosts of Misthaven Light?"

Ella cast a glance toward the lighthouse, now just a dark, brooding outline against the dimming sky. "I believe we might," she confessed, a note of uncertainty in her voice. "And I'm not sure whether that's thrilling or downright terrifying."

"I know what you mean," Benjamin responded, his hand reaching out to squeeze hers in a gesture of solidarity. He shivered, as if the cool air carried more than just the night's chill. "Whatever happens, tonight brings some kind of closure."

Hand in hand, they strolled towards the canopied area set up for the dinner break. Joining them was Ashlyn, whose quiet presence seemed to offer a comforting balance. The tingle of excitement mixed with apprehension within Ella grew stronger.

The dinner unfolded with lively chatter. Crew members exchanged theories and guesses about the potential encounters of the night. Despite the cheerful banter, an undercurrent of eager anticipation ran beneath it all. As darkness enveloped the area, the lighthouse stood silent and imposing, a guardian of history and secrets.

After the meal, as they prepared to resume the investigation, Ella noticed a distinct shift in the crew's mood. The earlier light-heartedness had now morphed into a focused determination as everyone geared up for the night's exploration. Catching her eye, Benjamin offered an encouraging nod, a silent message that they were in this together, whatever the night might reveal.

CHAPTER TEN

Memories in the Mist

Night descended upon them, shrouding the light-house and its surroundings in a cloak of mystery. The air was thick with anticipation, and the glow of lanterns and flashlights emanated from the lighthouse, casting long, haunting shadows across the team's path. As the equipment beeped to life and cameras started rolling, an energy wove through the group, binding them in shared purpose. They stood on the threshold of unveiling the hidden tales of Misthaven Light.

Ella leaned in, her voice a whisper. "Are you ready?"

Benjamin met her gaze. "As much as I can be." He paused, his expression softening. "How are you feeling?"

She hesitated for a beat, then confessed, "Terrified, excited, overwhelmed? Take your pick."

He chuckled. "Well, you're not alone in this. Remember that."

Just as she was about to respond, Trevor's voice cut through their conversation. "Alright, team, it's time!"

They turned, attention captured by Martin as he prepared for the opening segment. He cleared his throat, his voice resonating with a gravity that seemed to pull the night closer. "Tonight, on Ghostly Chronicles, we peer into the heart of Misthaven Light's past. This lighthouse, with its distinctive architecture, is a vessel of history and mystery alike."

With the introduction paving their way, the team ventured into the former abode of the lighthouse keepers. The moment Ella crossed the threshold, a sudden chill whispered across her skin, her body responding with an involuntary shiver.

It was Ashlyn who broke the silence. "To any spirits dwelling here, we seek your blessing to explore this place. We invite you to share your stories with us. To aid in our communication, we've arranged several tools throughout the grounds."

She gestured towards a table laden with an assortment of devices, each chosen with purpose. "This," she began, pointing to a small, box-like device, "is an EVP recorder. It can capture your voice, even if we can't hear you with our ears. Feel free to speak into it."

Next, she moved to a series of sensors spread across the room. "These are motion sensors and temperature gauges. Should you pass by them or affect the surrounding air, we'll know. It's a way for you to let us know of your presence without having to manifest."

Then Ashlyn showcased a modified radio, its static-filled airwaves slicing through the silence. "And this is a spirit box. It scans through radio frequencies rapidly, allowing you to form words or sentences. It's quite effective for real-time communication."

With the stage set, the atmosphere within the lighthouse keepers' residence thickened, charged with the energy of both the living and the ethereal. The team stood ready to bridge the gap between worlds while outside. Meanwhile, the soft murmur of the sea against the cliffs outside seemed to whisper secrets, urging them deeper into the mysteries of Misthaven Light.

The entire process turned out to be way less exciting than Ella had imagined. Once they had everything set, the night kinda just... slowed down. They ended up sitting around in a hush, the quiet that makes you aware of every little sound, like the creak of the old lighthouse floors or someone's stomach growling.

Every so often, the EMF meter would beep or flash, slicing through the boredom. Someone would toss out a comment like, "Oh, must be the wiring," or a hopeful, "Hey, maybe it's our ghostly host?" But after the first few times, even that lost its novelty.

The thrill of maybe, just maybe, catching a ghost on tape had morphed into a waiting game. A game of who could sit still the longest without checking their phone or, in Benjamin's case, becoming so quiet you'd almost forget he was there.

Ella tried to stay focused, but her mind kept drifting—until, out of nowhere, she'd get this tingle at the back of her neck. The air would feel different, cooler, maybe, or just... charged. Each time that happened, she'd snap to attention, scanning the room, half expecting to see someone standing in the corner. But then, nothing would happen, and the moment would pass, leaving her to wonder if it was all in her head.

As the night crawled on, with everyone sort of lost in their own world of boredom or quiet contemplation, Ella couldn't shake off the feeling that they weren't alone. Not in a spooky, there's-a-ghost-right-behind-you way, but more like a subtle nudge, a gentle hint that someone was just out of sight, watching.

During one of those quiet moments, Ella leaned towards Ashlyn. "I think Nathaniel is near. Like, really near." She didn't know if it was wishful thinking or something more, but now and then, she felt a presence similar to the intensity of her dreams.

Benjamin, still as a statue, gave nothing away. But Ella couldn't help but feel that, in his silence, he was sensing something too, maybe even more than the rest of them.

Ashlyn, with a look of deep focus shadowing her features, leaned in closer to the heart of their makeshift command center. Her hushed voice seemed to carry weight in the silence. "Nathaniel is here... I can feel him around us."

The team, caught in a moment of anticipation, adjusted their positions, ensuring the infrared cameras were angled to capture the unseen. Martin, with a nod, initiated the EVP (Electronic Voice Phenomenon) session with a steadiness in his voice. "Nathaniel, if you're among us, could you give us any sign of your presence?"

A moment passed, heavy with expectation, before Travis chimed in. "Nathaniel, if it's Isabella you wish to reach, do you have a message for her? Anything at all?"

The air within the room seemed to drop a few degrees, the only sounds filling the void being the mechanical hum of their equipment and the rhythmic, distant crash of waves against the cliffs. Question after question was posed, met with silence or the soft, ambiguous responses of their devices until Lydia, with a practiced motion, halted the recording to review the evidence they had collected.

Everyone leaned in, a collective breath held as the playback crackled to life, their ears tuned for the faintest hint of the otherworldly. And there it was, clear in the static after Travis's inquiry—a soft whisper that sent a shiver through the room. "Isabella."

The response was like a jolt, electrifying the stagnant air. Ella felt a chill creep down her spine as she sought Benjamin's hand for comfort. Misthaven Light, with its storied past and shadowed halls, was sharing its tale.

Throughout the night's vigil, Benjamin's presence had shifted, his usual attentiveness dimming into an uncharacteristic quietude. Ella couldn't help but notice the change. It hung between them, an invisible veil that had altered their dynamic.

As they moved from room to room, Benjamin trailed behind, his steps deliberate, almost hesitant. His gaze often drifted to distant corners, lingering on shadows that seemed no different to Ella. Yet, it was as if he saw something beyond the mundane, something that held his attention with an invisible grip.

Ella watched him, concern knitting her brow. At moments, he seemed to start at a sound only he could hear, his head tilting, as if straining to catch a noise carried on the air. His responses to her, when she reached out to him with a question or a comment, came slower, as if he were pulling his attention back from far away.

The decision to move closer to the spot where Isabella had fallen caused Ella to feel some unease. As the ghost hunting crew carried their equipment, the waning moon's light cast a haunting glow on the clifftop.

The moment Ella stepped outside, memories of Isabella's tragic fate washed over her. Her breath hitched, and a paralyzing fear gripped her. It felt as though she was being pulled towards the cliff's edge. She reached out to Benjamin again, but he had fallen behind.

Martin, sensing the intensity of the moment, took a deep breath and began addressing the camera. "Legend speaks of Isabella's tragic demise right here on this very cliff. A heartbroken soul, she plummeted to the waves below. Tonight, we hope to connect with her spirit, and perhaps bring solace to the lingering anguish that surrounds this spot."

Ashlyn closed her eyes, her fingertips touching the ground as if grounding herself. The team waited with bated breath as Martin called out, "Isabella, we come in peace, hoping to hear your story. Can you communicate with us?" When they listened back on the recorder, all they heard was silence.

Switching gears, Travis took a different approach. "Nathaniel, if you're here with us, could you give us a sign?" The reply was the same, just the gentle, melancholic touch of the breeze brushing against them.

The atmosphere felt heavier, as if the air itself was charged with a silent, watchful presence. Ashlyn broke through the growing tension, her voice brusque. "Stay sharp, everyone. There's something off here, a kind of dark presence among us."

"Maybe we should try the spirit box?" Lydia suggested, cutting through the unease with a practical solution. The idea was met with nods, and she set about preparing the device.

As the spirit box hummed to life, scanning through frequencies with a soft crackle, Travis proposed. "Let's attempt to reach out to Samuel. He was rumored to have murdered Isabella. Adding the headset might make it more direct."

All eyes shifted to Benjamin. Travis added, "Having a familial connection might just make our attempt more potent."

Benjamin hesitated before he agreed. "Okay, but if things get too intense, pull me out, promise?"

With the headphones set, Benjamin became a focal point of their circle, a bridge to the unseen, illuminated by the soft glow of the moon. Travis initiated the contact, "Samuel, if your spirit is with us, please communicate through Benjamin."

The night's stillness was punctuated by the static of the spirit box. Travis, his face illuminated by the glow of the equipment, continued his line of questioning, directing it towards Samuel. "Samuel, if you are here with us, please give us a sign. Why has this tragedy persisted over the years?"

Static buzzed with no answer.

Then Benjamin's voice, hollow yet clear, cut through, "The curse on the Blackwoods... forever." Ella felt a shift in her perception, as if reality was warping. The voices of the crew grew faint, their words echoing as though she was listening from underwater. A mysterious pull tugged at her, guiding her towards the cliff's edge. It was an involuntary lure, like a moth drawn to the flame.

Clarity flickered in and out. Benjamin's figure anchored these fleeting moments, his voice now distant and altered, laden with resentment. "Blackwood betrayed me... took everything... The curse shall never end." The others' voices turned into mere background noise, like flies buzzing, easy to ignore.

"How did Blackwood betray Samuel?..."

"It wasn't Samuel... It was Elias Thorton.."

"Those remains we found... Why didn't we connect the dots sooner?"

As the wind whipped through her hair and the salty scent of the sea intensified, Ella's awareness of her surroundings sharpened, alerting her to her position on the cliff. She noticed Benjamin's stiff posture, his gaze fixed on something distant, his voice echoing the pain and betrayal.

From afar, she heard Ashlyn's alarmed shout. Was it her name she was calling? "Ella!" It sounded urgent and worried.

But the call of the cliff was stronger, more insistent, urging her to come closer. A chill spread through her limbs, a sensation like icy fingers wrapping around her heart.

Somewhere, she registered Travis's horrified expression as he pieced together who they were communicating with. Martin was scrambling, papers rustling. But their actions were overshadowed by the compulsion, that undeniable urge leading her to the edge.

Flashes of Benjamin's face flitted through her consciousness—the same features, yet contorted.

A sudden warmth enveloped her wrist, breaking through the haze. Benjamin, or was it Elias, holding her back? Or perhaps trying to pull her further?

She tried to focus, to ground herself. But the world around her was spinning, a chaotic whirl of voices, sensations, and emotions. She was on the precipice, teetering between the past's pull and the present's desperate pleas.

She tried to summon words, but her voice wavered, caught by fear and uncertainty. "Benjamin? Is it you in there?"

His response was a murmur, words layered with bitterness. "Not entirely." His fingers clamped around her wrist, their icy touch cutting through her like a winter's chill.

Desperation surged through her. "Benjamin, fight it," she pleaded, seeking the familiar warmth in his eyes.

For a split second, agony played across his face, and in a voice quivering with effort, he uttered, "Ella... run."

CHAPTER ELEVEN

Whispers of the Future

Without thinking, she braced to run away from Benjamin, but he held tight. "She won't be leaving," came his venomous whisper, his breath now exuding a stench of rot.

Chills raced down Ella's spine. The atmosphere became suffocating, the cold pressing into her, making each breath a labor. She seized a fleeting burst of adrenaline, jerked her wrist free, and broke into a sprint, her heart pounding in tandem with her echoing footfalls. She dared not glance over her shoulder, but the prickling sensation told her he—or whatever had consumed him—would be close.

Ella's heartbeat thundered in her ears as she sped towards the cliff, the wind biting at her cheeks and tossing her hair into a chaotic dance. The silvery sheen of the moonlit path lit her way, the mischievous play of shadows threatening to trip her up at every step. Yet, she forged ahead.

The rhythmic crashing of the waves below crescendoed, calling out to her like a siren as she heard Benjamin's footsteps. They seemed distorted and out of place.

Just then, second set of steps and a voice cut through the night. It was Ashlyn, chasing them, her voice unwavering as she chanted a protection prayer. The words melded with the night, creating a shield. "By the light and the might, ward away the shadow's blight. Guard this soul, keep it whole, let the darkness take no toll."

Tears clouded Ella's vision, yet she didn't wipe them away. With each step, an inexplicable pull beckoned her closer to the cliff's edge, as if the land itself demanded her presence. She could no longer distinguish whether she was fleeing or being drawn to the precipice. Her body moved as if under the command of another. The sharp, briny scent of salt filled her nostrils, while the constant roar of the waves smashing against the cliff's base wove a haunting melody that seemed to both warm and welcome her.

But before she could reach safety, Benjamin overtook her. A chilling, iron-like grip clamped down on her shoulder. There he stood, his eyes devoid of any warmth blocking her path.

Just as despair was on the verge of engulfing Ella, a sudden comfort wrapped around her, piercing the icy dread. It was as if Nathaniel's spirit had materialized from the ether, his presence a hope in the darkness. He emerged beside her, his form coalescing from wisps of mist into a more solid figure, countering the malevolence emanating from the possessed Benjamin For a fleeting moment, time seemed to pause, the air charged with tension as the two forces—Nathaniel's spirit and the dark entity controlling Benjamin—engaged in a silent, metaphysical tug-of-war.

Benjamin's grip faltered under Nathaniel's influence, his fingers slackening as if the ghost's presence sapped the force of its power. Seizing the moment, Ella wrenched free, stumbling backwards. She drew in sharp, ragged gasps, her lungs burning for air after the terror-induced constriction.

As she regained her footing, Ella witnessed a spectacle that would forever alter her understanding of the world. Nathaniel, his visage glowing with light, stood firm against Benjamin, who appeared tormented, caught between his own consciousness and the dark will forcing its command upon him. Nathaniel's face was a mask of resolve, yet it bore a serene expression.

"Nathaniel?" Ella's voice was a whisper. The ghost turned towards her, his eyes conveying a depth of sorrow and determination. It was a look that spoke of battles fought in realms beyond her comprehension, of a love that transcended the boundaries of life and death.

"I'm here to protect you, Isabella," Nathaniel's voice resonated around her, a soothing balm. "But we must act with haste. He is not himself, and the darkness within him seeks to consume all it touches."

Ella's mind reeled at the name—Isabella. *I am not Isabella;* she thought. *Nathaniel never loved me.*

Ashlyn burst into the fray, her long coat trailing behind her like the wings of an avenging angel. "Ella!" she shouted, her voice breaking through the spectral standoff. Her outstretched hand was both an offer of safety and a desperate plea.

From the corner of her eye, Ella noticed the rest ghost hunting crew sprinting towards them, their faces full of fear and fascination. "Is this even real?" the cameraman yelled, his eyes darting between the two apparitions. "Is the camera catching this?" the other one shouted, adjusting the lens.

"Stay back!" Ella's voice cut through the air. "Stay away from him!"

Nathaniel and the spirit in Benjamin's body faced off. Their struggle was manifesting in the very fabric of the environment. The ground quivered beneath their feet, as if echoing their battle, while the sea mirrored their strife, waves crashing against the rocks below.

Ashlyn's voice rose above the chaos, clear and strong. Her hands moved, tracing symbols in the air as she began an incantation, a spell of separation.

"By the powers of the earth and sea, I command thee, release Benjamin and be free!"

Benjamin's body convulsed as if caught in a violent storm. His voice, echoing both the malice and his own terror, screamed out in agony. Ashlyn persisted, sweat beading on her forehead, her focus unwavering.

"Nathaniel, stand with us! Aid in this man's release and bring peace!"

Benjamin, with Ashlyn's guidance and the residual strength of Nathaniel's protective energy, fought against Elias. With a deafening scream, the entity was expelled from Benjamin's form, its shadowy essence clashing with Nathaniel in a blinding explosion of light. Before this, everyone had been certain the killer had been was Samuel, yet the truth unfurled most unexpectedly, revealing Elias Thornton as the true vessel for the malevolent presence.

The moment the spirit began its departure from Benjamin, the surroundings took on an eerie calm. It was as though the earth itself held its breath, anticipating the inevitable clash between Nathaniel and Elias. The sky, previously a clear canvas, morphed into a tumultuous sea of clouds. Cracks appeared, not with the sound of shattering glass but with the ominous silence of a world holding back its fury. From these fissures, a vortex of swirling energies emerged, commanding attention.

The sky above them opened, a vortex of swirling energies, with Nathaniel and Elias caught in its eye. Their bodies radiated, casting shadows that danced around them. They clashed above, ascending towards the heavens in a duel that seemed to defy the laws of nature itself.

This was no mere fight. It was a dance of destiny, a ballet of the damned. Each movement was charged, each strike a sentence in the story of their eternal struggle. Bolts of energy, raw and untamed, darted between them, illuminating the sky with their brilliance. Below, the world seemed to fade into insignificance, a mere backdrop to the cataclysm above.

When the brilliance faded, both Elias and Nathaniel were gone. The sky returned to its inky blackness, the stars twinkling as if they'd witnessed a legend unfold.

Benjamin, exhausted, collapsed to the ground, unconscious. Ashlyn, also spent from the ordeal, knelt by his side, placing her hand on his shoulder. The crew, their faces full of awe, moved closer, forgetting their equipment in the aftermath of the extraordinary events they had witnessed.

Ella felt a deep sorrow tightening around her heart, each beat sending ripples throughout her body. Nathaniel's fleeting image, now just a spectral memory in the sky, seemed to tug at her soul. Tears traced glistening paths down her cheeks. With each step she took, the sound of gravel underfoot echoed the sadness she carried.

"Is he... has Nathaniel left us?" Ella's voice trembled with emotion.

Ashlyn, drained by the night's events, looked up, following Ella's gaze toward the heavens. "In essence," she murmured, a note of sadness in her whisper. "I think what's left is an echo, a lingering vestige of his presence."

Her grief almost overwhelmed Ella, but then the sight of Benjamin, still on the ground, sparked a rush of concern within her. She hurried to his side, caressing his face in a gesture of comfort.

"Benjamin?" she whispered.

"He's going to be alright," Ashlyn said. "The ordeal of possession and its release has drained him, but he'll recover."

Ella responded with a nod, her arms encircling Benjamin.

Martin and Trevor approached, concern on their faces. It was Trevor who broke the silence. "Ash, I've been in this field for years, but I've never encountered anything this intense."

Ashlyn paused, as if absorbing the residual energy of their surroundings. "Love wields incredible power," she stated, glancing at the recovering Benjamin. "Our work here isn't finished. There are still many spirits eager to share their stories."

Martin inquired, ready to assist. "Should I gather the rest of the crew?"

Ella gave a nod of agreement, aware of their commitment to this journey. The crew had been accommodating, and it was only fair to include them. "Yes, but let's spare Benjamin the indignity of being filmed while he is passed out. He wouldn't appreciate that."

Martin chuckled in understanding and nodded in agreement.

In the shadow of the towering lighthouse, under the blanket of stars, Ashlyn gathered the group in a semi-circle on the rugged ground. The sea's roar provided a mournful soundtrack to the night's solemn proceedings. With only the moonlight, to illuminate their faces.

Ashlyn took a moment to address the circle, her voice calm and clear. "The spirits will speak through me tonight. I will not be conversing with them directly. If you have questions, or seek clarity on whom we're speaking with, you must ask. I'll be the vessel for their voices."

With the group's understanding, Ashlyn closed her eyes, her posture relaxed yet focused. A tense silence enveloped the gathering.

Soon, Ashlyn's demeanor changed, her facial expressions and posture reflecting someone else's presence. "I... I pushed her," a whisper carried by the wind filled the silence. "Isabella... it was an accident. Elias... he had taken hold of me. I would never harm her. She was like a sister to me, and her betrothed..." Ashlyn's voice trailed off, choked by unrequited love and despair. "I couldn't leave, not with this guilt."

"Who is this?" Ella asked.

Ashlyn, still under the influence of the spirit, replied, "Samuel."

The group absorbed Samuel's tragic confession, the air heavy with his centuries-old guilt.

"Can you find peace, knowing your remorse is acknowledged, and that we know you did not do it?" Benjamin ventured, his question directed at Samuel through Ashlyn.

The atmosphere shifted, a silent sign of Samuel's response, his spirit finding solace in the acknowledgment of his pain.

Ashlyn's expression changed again, softening as a fresh voice emerged. "I moved on too swiftly after Elias was lost to the sea," she expressed with a tone of sorrow and regret.

"Who are we speaking with now?" Martin asked, trying to piece together the historical puzzle.

"Clara. Marrying Blackwood was a mistake. I'm sorry, Elias," Ashlyn conveyed, the spirit of Clara seeking forgiveness through her confession.

As the evening progressed, Isabella and Nathaniel's spirits also found voice through Ashlyn, their words woven with the deep sorrow of a love and life unfulfilled. The group, now familiar with the process, asked questions, guiding the conversation to unearth the stories and sentiments of the lingering souls.

Beneath the canopy of stars, time seemed to stand still. With each spirit's confession and farewell, a sense of healing wove its way through the hearts of the living and the departed alike. The night air, once thick with untold stories and pent-up regrets, grew lighter, infused with whispers of forgiveness and the silent strength of closure.

It was as if the very essence of the lighthouse, witness to years of solitude and sorrow, now radiated a soft glow of reconciliation and peace. And then, as subtly as the night had embraced them in its shadowy fold, the first hints of dawn edged on the horizon. The transition was almost imperceptible at first, a gentle lightening of the sky that went unnoticed as the group lingered in the emotional aftermath of their spiritual journey. Yet, as the hues shifted from the deep indigo of night to the softer shades of morning, reality nudged its way back.

Around Ella, the crew moved in a daze, gathering equipment and exchanging murmured conversations. Their faces mirrored a melange of wonder, exhaustion, and profound relief.

Ashlyn, her voice hoarse from the evening's events, broke the pensive silence. "Never, in all my encounters with the supernatural, have I witnessed such an intense commingling of past and present." Her gaze rested on Ella, carrying a silent message of understanding. "The spirits tonight, Nathaniel above all, were drawn to the raw emotion tethering the past to the now."

Ella's gaze drifted towards the sea, each wave whispering ancient tales. A soft touch on her shoulder prompted her to turn. Benjamin stood there, his usual confidence dimmed by a hint of vulnerability. "I only remember bits and pieces of... you know, when I wasn't myself," he said, his voice shaking. "But the thought that I could've hurt you, even without meaning to, it's getting to me."

Ella slipped her fingers through his, offering comfort. "We were both caught up in it. I felt more like Isabella than myself, honestly." She nodded towards the lighthouse and suggested with a soft smile, "How about we grab some breakfast?"

It was then that she felt it. That all too familiar prickle at the nape of her neck. Turning, she stared at Nathaniel's waning silhouette, its translucence resembling the light of dawn. Their eyes met.

Benjamin stood next to her, squeezing her hand.

Nathaniel's voice, though faint, was unmistakable. "Isabella."

A surge of emotions threatened to break Ella. Tears blurred her vision as she reached out, hoping against hope to grasp the essence of a love lost in time. As the figure of Nathaniel dissolved, his smile left behind a silent adieu, etched forever into her soul.

They reconvened with the others beneath the breakfast canopy, where tables were laden with assorted pastries. But more crucial than the tempting array of baked goods was the coffee! Steaming pots promised to revive their spirits. This was an elixir that seemed more precious than gold in the soft light of the morning.

Ella traced the rim of her coffee mug, her mind a whirlpool of memories and emotions. Every time she closed her eyes, she saw Nathaniel, and faint whispers of 'Isabella' echoed in the wind. But the scent of warm toast and butter grounded her back to the present, to reality, to Benjamin.

Her gaze shifted to meet his. His eyes, while lit by the morning sun, bore exhaustion from the previous night. The unspoken bond, the shared experience, linked them in that moment. As the silence stretched, she ventured, "What happens now to the spirits we spoke to?"

Ashlyn answered, her voice softer than the rustle of leaves. "It's up to them. I felt both Samuel and Clara were at peace, and I believe they have moved on. As for Isabella, I still feel a whisper, same as Nathaniel. It's as if their souls still seek each other, even as echoes. They may never leave, but at least they are safe spirits."

Ella felt a pang in her heart. "Star-crossed lovers," she murmured. "Bound by fate, but forever separated."

Benjamin, sensing her melancholy, reached over, his warm hand enveloping hers. "Their tale is a good reminder," he began, "that we must seize the moments given to us and cherish those we share them with."

Ashlyn added, "Every soul has a tale, every echo a lament. They yearn to be remembered."

"Why do I feel this all so deeply?" Ella asked.

Ashlyn, looking thoughtful, replied. "Your experiences are bigger than just the echoes of trauma. Your dreams, these visions, are touched by something more. Psychic inclinations can be genetic."

Ella furrowed her brow, perplexed. "You really think Isabella is related to me?"

"Think of family lines as streams that carry echoes," Ashlyn explained. "These can be memories, emotions, or even talents. Your connection with Isabella could go much deeper than we thought. Perhaps she is an ancestor of yours. This bond, enhanced by your inherent psychic sensitivity, could be the reason your experiences seem so vivid."

Benjamin, looking bemused, chimed in, "So, what you're saying is, Ella's dreams could be ancestral memories?"

Ashlyn nodded, "Precisely, similar to your experiences with Samuel. They're reverberations from the past, touching Ella because of her psychic predisposition and potentially a familial connection."

Overwhelmed, Ella settled onto the ground. "That's a lot to process."

"It is," Ashlyn agreed, her smile warm. "But it's beautiful that you and Benjamin have found each other. You truly are kindred spirits."

Together, they sat in silent contemplation; the ocean stretching before them, its waves a gentle hymn to the continuity of life and connections beyond time.

As the midday sun cast its golden rays over the island, Ella stood on the deck of the boat, the gentle hum of the engine and the occasional cry of seabirds filling the air. The island, with its beautiful lighthouse, receded into the distance. The night before felt like a dream, its edges already blurring in her memory, yet the emotions it evoked were as vivid as ever.

Beside her, Benjamin was quiet, his gaze fixed on the shrinking silhouette of the lighthouse. The ritual had left an indelible mark on both their hearts. It was a shared experience, unique and profound, binding them in ways neither understood yet.

Ella's mind replayed the events of the previous night—the overwhelming sense of Nathaniel's love for Isabella, the sorrow of their unfulfilled lives, and the catharsis of their last goodbye. It was as if she had lived through a love story centuries old, feeling every moment of joy and heartache as her own.

The realization that she might share a bloodline with Isabella, as suggested by Ashlyn, added layers of complexity to her reflections. It wasn't just the psychic sensitivity that linked her to the past; it was the possibility of a familial connection spanning generations. This revelation made the island's history not just a curiosity but a part of her own story, a chapter of her ancestry that had been waiting to be uncovered.

Turning to Benjamin, she noticed the thoughtful expression on his face. "You're quiet," she said, breaking the silence between them.

He turned to her, a soft smile playing on his lips. "I was just thinking about Nathaniel and Isabella. About how, in the end, they found some semblance of peace. It's a powerful reminder of how love can transcend time, even in the face of tragedy."

Ella nodded, her eyes returning to the island. In her heart, she felt hope, a belief that the spirits of Nathaniel and Isabella were no longer bound by the sorrow that had tethered them to the lighthouse. Instead, she imagined them hand in hand, free to watch over the island together, their love a beacon as enduring as the lighthouse itself.

As the island faded from view, Ella felt a sense of closure, not just for the spirits, but for herself as well. The experience had changed her, deepening her understanding of her own abilities and opening her heart to the complexities of love and loss.

She turned to Benjamin, taking his hand in hers. "Let's promise to never forget this," she said, her voice steady and sure. "Let's keep the memory of Nathaniel and Isabella alive, as a reminder of what we've experienced and how it's brought us closer."

Benjamin squeezed her hand in response, his agreement silent but unequivocal. Together, they watched as the island disappeared on the horizon, a chapter closing behind them, leaving them to navigate the uncharted waters of their own future, strengthened by the past and the love that had revealed itself in the most unexpected of ways.

Ella stepped into the living room. The scent of pine and of sea salt lingered in the air and the gentle clink of her glass setting on the coffee table broke the silence. Benjamin, seated at the nearby desk, looked up from his laptop, his face breaking into a smile.

"Guess what Captain did today?" Ella began, a playful tone in her voice as she sank into the armchair.

Benjamin raised an eyebrow, closing his laptop. "What mischief has our fearless explorer gotten into now?"

"He decided that the neighbor's garden was the perfect place to bury his new toy. Mrs. Henderson was not amused." Ella chuckled, shaking her head. The Labrador in question, Captain, lay at her feet, offering a guilty but unrepentant wag of his tail.

"That dog has more adventure in him than most people," Benjamin laughed, standing up to join Ella, bending down to ruffle Captain's ears. "Speaking of adventures, today marks a year since our island journey."

Ella's eyes lit up, the memory sparking a warmth in her heart. "A year already? It feels like both a lifetime ago and just yesterday."

Benjamin nodded, his gaze softening. "It changed everything, didn't it? Speaking of changes," he shifted the topic, "the book's doing better than I could've dreamed. It's resonating with people, Ella. Our story, the history of the island, Nathaniel and Isabella's love... it's touching hearts."

Ella's smile widened. "I'm so proud of you, Ben. And... I have some news too. The gallery's ribbon-cutting is scheduled for next month. The invites went out today."

"Your own gallery," Benjamin mused, his voice filled with admiration. "Your art deserves this spotlight, Ella. Those beautiful scenes... they're a window to your soul."

Their eyes met, an acknowledgment of the journey they had shared, the love that had grown, and the future they were building together.

"You know," Benjamin began, a slight nervousness creeping into his voice, "I've been thinking a lot about our future, about us. And I can't imagine a day without you."

Ella's heart skipped a beat. Captain, perhaps sensing it too, lifted his head, his eyes darting between them.

Benjamin knelt down, not just to be closer to Captain, but to bridge the small space between him and Ella. From his pocket, he pulled out a small velvet box.

"Ella, will you marry me?"

Tears of joy welled in Ella's eyes, mirroring the sparkling diamond that lay nestled in the box. "Yes, Benjamin," she whispered, her voice steady despite the whirlwind of emotions. "Yes, I will."

As they embraced, Captain's joyful bark filled the room, a seal of approval from their furry family member. Outside, the setting sun cast a golden glow, a perfect backdrop to a new chapter in their story.

Their journey had begun with a dream, a vision that pulled Ella from the other side of the country to a destiny she could have never imagined. It was a call intertwined with spirits and past love, and to Benjamin. Now, as they looked toward the future, their path was lit not only by the experiences they shared but also by the spirits that first brought them together. The warmth of their home, the adventures that lay ahead, and the unbreakable bond of their love were all beacons of light shining on the journey that lay before them.

Afterword

Growing up, my dad was this amazing mix of historian and teacher, while my mom was all about cheering on my every wild idea. Childhood was this cool mash-up of creativity and diving deep into history. It wasn't the big, headline-grabbing events that grabbed me. The personal stories were the ones that caught my interest.

My family's open-mindedness lent itself to a curiosity about lesser-known lore. I couldn't get enough of the stories that simmered in the background, whispered rather than proclaimed.

That curiosity? It just grew with me. I found out that ghost tours are like this secret doorway into the parts of history that are a bit more... shadowy. They're this perfect mix of real historical facts and the supernatural stories that give you goosebumps. The best tour guides? They know exactly how to walk that fine line between what's real and what's just a great story.

So, the whole Kindred Spirits Mystery series idea? It hit me during one of those tours. Each book is going to pull from a ghost story. The way each story connects might change, but they all dive into these cool historical mysteries and the spirits that might still hang around.

I grew up in New England, which is a treasure trove of stories. Trying to pick just one is impossible. So, I dreamed up Misthaven Island. It's a bit like Egg Rock Island in Maine, and a bunch of other light house islands, all rolled into one. It's our fictional spot to explore bits and pieces from some of Maine's most haunted lighthouses.

I'm hoping that as you dive into the Kindred Spirits Mysteries, you'll get as excited as I am about exploring where history and the supernatural meet. These stories are your invitation to get curious, to explore, and maybe open your mind a bit to what might be out there. Thanks for coming along on this adventure with me.

About the Author

Beth Connor is a weaver of tales, captivated by writing and fueled by a love for storytelling.

Beth's creative pursuits are a reflection of her life philosophy, and she is always searching for new ways to expand her knowledge and understanding of the world. She has a keen eye for detail and a remarkable ability to create vivid, dynamic settings that resonate with her audience.

Beth's talent has earned her recognition as the author of several published works, including the captivating novels "Hollow City" and The Isdralan Chronicles Series as well as a contributor to many anthologies. Beth is also an accomplished audiobook narrator and the host of the popular podcast, "Crossroads Cantina."

Despite her many endeavors, Beth remains down-to-earth and dedicated to living authentically, true to her passions and values. She resides in the Pacific Northwest with her husband, two children, and canine companions, who bring her boundless inspiration and delight.

Also by

ALSO BY BETH CONNOR:

Hollow City

<u>The Isdralan Chronicles:</u>
Micah and the Candles of Time
Prodigy of Flame
Bridge of Blood and Thornes

<u>Kindred Spirit Mysteries:</u>
The Secret of Misthaven Island
Bridging the Heart